THE EYE OF
MIDNIGHT

THE EYE OF MIDNIGHT

ANDREW BRUMBACH

DELACORTE PRESS

Text copyright © 2016 by Andrew Brumbach
Jacket art copyright © 2016 by Jeff Nentrup

All rights reserved. Published in the United States by Delacorte Press, an imprint of Random House Children's Books, a division of Penguin Random House LLC, New York. The excerpt of *Disputatio regalis et nobilissimi iuvenis Pippini cum Albino scholastico* that appears on pages 129–130 was translated into English by the author.

Delacorte Press is a registered trademark and the colophon is a trademark of Penguin Random House LLC.

Visit us on the Web! randomhousekids.com

Educators and librarians, for a variety of teaching tools, visit us at RHTeachersLibrarians.com

Library of Congress Cataloging-in-Publication Data
Brumbach, Andrew, author.
The eye of midnight / Andrew Brumbach. — First edition.
pages cm
Summary: In May 1929 Maxine Campbell and her cousin William Battersea arrive at their grandfather's house in New Jersey to find that the house is empty—and soon they are caught up in the contest for an ancient Arabian relic called the Eye of Midnight, which several secret societies are willing to do anything to posses.
ISBN 978-0-385-74461-4 (hc) — ISBN 978-0-385-39069-9 (ebook) — ISBN 978-0-375-99176-9 (glb) 1. Antiquities—Juvenile fiction. 2. Secret societies—Juvenile fiction. 3. Cousins—Juvenile fiction. 4. Grandfathers—Juvenile fiction. 5. Adventure stories. 6. New York (N.Y.)—History—1898–1951—Juvenile fiction. [1. Antiquities—Fiction. 2. Secret societies—Fiction. 3. Cousins—Fiction. 4. Grandfathers—Fiction. 5. Adventure and adventurers—Fiction. 6. New York (N.Y.)—History—1898–1951—Fiction.] I. Title.
PZ7.1.B8Ey 2016
[Fic]—dc23
2015004177

The text of this book is set in 12.25-point Goudy.
Jacket design by Kate Gartner
Interior design by Heather Kelly

Printed in the United States of America
10 9 8 7 6 5 4 3 2 1
First Edition

For Jacob, Drew, Davis, and Ruby,
my pride and joy

You who must travel with a weary load
Along this darkling, labyrinthine street—
I have men with torches at your head and feet
If you would pass the dangers of the road.

—the Diwan of Abu'l-ala al-Maarri

PROLOGUE

NEW YORK CITY

MAY 19, 1929

The hour has come, called the voice of the master.

The Hashashin watched from his place in the shadows, staring out into the sunlit street.

"I am a living dagger," he replied in a hoarse whisper, "thrust by the Old Man's hand." He pressed three fingers to his forehead and made a low bow.

Across the street, the door of the telegraph office swung open, and a heavy, grizzle-bearded man emerged, tucking an envelope into his pocket as he started up the block. The Hashashin followed quickly, stepping from his concealment into the street amid the coughing, growling motorcars.

The strangeness of this place still unbalanced him, and it was more than these lurching machines in the road. The customs and laws of this country were alien; the speech was difficult. His garments felt awkward and uncomfortable—

the coat and trousers, the necktie at his throat, the brimmed hat pulled low over his eyes.

All this was of no consequence, of course. He reached into his coat and found his knife, felt the edge sticky-sharp beneath his thumb, felt the certainty of its weight in his palm.

Up ahead, the sacrifice moved at an easy pace, pausing to take in the window displays of several shops along the way. The Hashashin held back, moving inconspicuously through the crowds with eyes fixed like barbed hooks on the back of the man's neck, until finally they arrived at a faded storefront squeezed between a butcher shop and a Chinese laundry, with a window lettered in flaking gold:

RUGS–CARPETS
→ANATOLIAN & PERSIAN←
FINEST QUALITY

The Hashashin waited while the man unlocked the entrance; then he circled the building and found a rear door. Producing a pair of slender steel instruments from a leather wallet, he picked the lock and slipped inside a dim storeroom, blinking twice as his eyes adjusted to the heavy darkness. A gray Persian cat, startled by his arrival, darted past him and disappeared down an aisle of wooden crates and baled rugs. The Hashashin paused and listened.

A steady string of thumps echoed faintly in the gloom. The Hashashin crept toward the sounds, weaving his way through the cluttered space like a jackal among the tombs, until he came at last to a standing row of rolled carpets at the back of a small showroom.

Except for the afternoon rays that filtered through the dusty windows, the store was unlit. It was the same back in the bazaars of far-off Baghdad and Istanbul. In this way the shops were kept tolerably cool even in the oppressive heat of midday. Only when a customer chanced to enter would the hot bulbs above be switched on, illuminating the rich carpets in a magnificent blaze of color.

There were no customers now. Here in the shadows, old grizzle-beard worked alone in the middle of the floor, heaving a pile of rugs back one by one with a whoosh and a thud, checking his inventory with a series of regular grunts. His task absorbed him entirely.

Like the rumble of distant thunder, the voice of the master called to the Hashashin from beyond the void.

His life is forfeit.

The Hashashin exhaled silently and drew his knife. In an instant, in the space between two heartbeats, the stroke would be accomplished.

"One breath more, *sadiqi*," he whispered as he started to step out into the room.

At that moment, the door of the shop opened, ringing a bell on the jamb. The carpet merchant looked up from his stack, and the Hashashin froze. Cursing silently, he shrank back into hiding.

"Mr. Constantin!" said a tall, gray-haired gentleman with a British accent.

"Ah, *effendi*," replied the carpet merchant, beaming. "Excellent timing, old friend! I am only just now returned."

The men shook hands, and the visitor removed his hat and smoothed his broad mustache.

"How are you these days? Business is good?"

"Tolerable," said Mr. Constantin with an indifferent wave.

The visitor nodded, sighing comfortably as he sank onto the pile of carpets. He ruffled his hair and stretched his arms. Then he stiffened.

"What is it?" asked Mr. Constantin. "Something is wrong?"

"I'm not sure." The visitor's eyes were alert now, probing. "You're alone?" he asked.

"Of course. Except for the cat. Perhaps you heard him chasing a mouse in the storeroom."

The Hashashin was seething inside, but he remained motionless. He had no instructions for this contingency. Perhaps both men should fall, though two strokes represented a more demanding test.

The visitor waited for several moments, listening for even the faintest disturbance of the stillness. None came. His senses chafed, unsatisfied, but at last he shook his head. "Has it arrived?"

Mr. Constantin nodded and handed him the telegram. "Do you have time for apple tea, Horatius?" he asked.

"Why not?" said his guest, turning his attention to the contents of the envelope. "I've never turned down tea before, that I recall."

As he scanned the lines, his jaw tightened in alarm.

"No," he murmured. "No . . . it can't be."

"Is everything all right?"

The gray-haired man hesitated, as if words momentarily failed him.

"The enemy has found them," he said. "After all these years . . ."

Mr. Constantin's eyes widened spectacularly. "And what of the Eye of Midnight?"

"The telegram mentions nothing on that point," muttered the visitor. "I'm sorry, but it looks as if I'll have to pass on tea. I have a train to catch."

He took up his hat and put his hand on the shopkeeper's shoulder, hastening for the door. "Thank you, old friend," he said in earnest, "and thank Yusuf for me as well."

Mr. Constantin shook his head. "It was nothing," he said. "The debt still stands on my side of the ledger, I think. Besides, I understand what this means to you. You know I would do anything to help."

His guest tipped his hat. "Tread carefully," he said. "The Old Man's arm is long."

Mr. Constantin made a circle with his thumb and forefinger and held it over his heart.

"Nothing will prevail," he said.

"The Cipher does not sleep," replied the gray-haired man, returning the peculiar salute as he turned for the door.

The Hashashin knew the visitor's identity and purpose now, knew also that his only opportunity to intercept the telegram had been lost.

Furiously, he tore open his garment and pressed the point of his blade to his chest. "I have failed the Old Man," he whispered.

Remember the command, rang the voice in his head. *Thy death belongs to me.*

His hand faltered and dropped to his side. He knew the creed. His life was not his own to take.

And yet, blood must still be spilled today.

Behind him, the gray cat crouched and hissed.

The Hashashin lifted his eyes toward the carpet merchant, who stood at the dusty window. He gripped his dagger and stepped out into the room.

CHAPTER 1

THE JERSEY SHORE

MAY 21, 1929

The weather turned dirty that first day, the day the cousins arrived in Hendon, back when the whole business was just at a beginning. A yellow taxicab rolled along under a canopy of dark clouds that blew in off the sea, and soon heavy drops began hammering the windshield, falling from a tombstone sky with such intense ill will it was hard to imagine that the sun could ever shine in this particular corner of the world.

The cab drove on, and the rain fell, and the miles slid past, until at last the car came to a stop, and a young girl no older than thirteen stepped out, ankle-deep, into a puddle. She pulled her suitcase from the back and paid the driver, who left her alone at the bottom of a hill.

Her gaze moved upward, past a formidable flight of steps, to a house atop a grassy perch that met her stare with a humorless frown, looking more like a fortress than a house, really—smooth stone; high, peaked roofs; and gables and towers beyond number. All something less than delightful, to her way of thinking. Not a flower to be seen, no cheerful curtains framing the dark windows, just a great gray edifice against a gray May sky.

She started up the hill, her suitcase bumping along behind her as she climbed the steps. Halfway to the top, she stopped and pushed the wet brown hair from her eyes.

"Just like Anne Boleyn climbing Tower Hill," she said under her breath, "right before she lost her head."

The image was tragically romantic, and she raised her chin with an air of somber dignity. Her suitcase had begun to feel like a load of wet sand, and for a moment she contemplated abandoning it there on the steps before finally resigning herself to her plight. Groaning wearily, she hefted the bag and pressed on.

By the time she reached the top of the stairs, she was soaked through. She looked back to the winding road that had brought her here. The taxicab was far away now, a yellow smudge in the distance.

She laid the back of her hand to her forehead and let out a mournful sigh, wondering how she looked.

Like a queen, she hoped. A desolate queen. Desolate but proud. And beautiful. Desolate and proud and beautiful. Watching the car vanish over the horizon, she drew a finger across her throat.

The rain was stinging now, but she no longer made any effort to cover her head. She took one last look up at the house and back down the long staircase, then turned to the great doorway before her, eyeing the bronze plate above the bell.

BATTERSEA MANOR, it read, and below that was a strange medallion figured with a single numeral—an elegantly engraved zero.

"What a strange address," she muttered to herself. "Welcome to the old family castle, Maxine. Such a lovely place to spend the summer."

She rang the bell and for a long time stood waiting on the doorstep. There was no answer or footfall within, so she rang again. Then, not knowing what else to do, she tried the knob. The door opened with a heavy groan, and she leaned through the crack, the end of her nose sluicing a steady stream of water onto the black-and-white tiles inside.

"Hello?" called Maxine. "Anybody?"

There was no reply.

The dry entry hall of a house, even a dark and cheerless one, struck Maxine as a vast improvement over a soggy front porch, and since the door was already open, she stepped across the threshold and glanced about.

"Grandpa?" she called. Then, as an afterthought, "Colonel Battersea?"

Her voice echoed down the dim hallway and died somewhere in the distant corners of the manor. The house seemed to be asleep, or perhaps lying in wait. Caesar's bust stared at her mutely from a pedestal beside the front staircase, and Maxine shivered as the puddle beneath her feet spread slowly across the tiled floor.

On the wall facing her was a tall blue mosaic framed by

a pointed stone arch. Judging by the carved basin set at the foot, it must have been a fountain once upon a time, set into a wall along a dusty street in some far-off place like Cairo or Algiers. The basin was dry now, and the exotic blue mosaic work had been fitted with brass hooks for jackets and hats. Maxine peeled off her wool coat and hung it there, where it dripped mournfully into the stone bath, and she decided she might as well have a look around.

The mansion was a labyrinth of winding corridors, and Maxine managed to lose herself several times without even leaving the first floor. She roamed the kitchen and the music room, the billiard room and the parlor, but all were empty and silent. The whole house, in fact, was as quiet as a tomb. The only sound at all came from an enormous grand-father clock in the entry hall—an ominous *tick-tock* that seemed to follow her from room to room and only served to heighten the stillness. She found herself tiptoeing, afraid to disturb the silence.

At length she came to a pair of double doors. Maxine paused for a moment, then grasped the handles and threw them wide, revealing a long, dark-paneled room inhabited by a great many books. A whole wall of them, in fact, on shelves the length of a train car, the highest of which could be reached only with the help of a wheeled ladder that rolled along on a track.

For some thirteen-year-olds, an afternoon in the library would have been more or less on par with a visit to the tai-lor's shop or an hour in the dentist's chair. Maxine, however, felt her spirits lift for the first time since she had arrived.

Her fingers brushed the spines as she walked the breadth of the room. The titles on the lower shelves were not entirely encouraging . . . Ovid's *Metamorphoses*, in fifteen volumes, sandwiched between Disraeli and Milton. Latin dictionaries and German medical books, encyclopedias and botanical folios. She wrinkled her nose at them, as if the pages harbored a colony of creeping parasites. Still, she felt sure there had to be something of interest here, and indeed, as her gaze drifted upward she began to take heart. Huck and Tom, Dr. Jekyll and Mr. Hyde, Long John Silver, the good-natured Mr. Toad—her old friends all regarded her from the upper shelves with silent goodwill.

The enormity of the collection presented certain difficulties, however. Maxine considered for a moment the proposition of trying to select a single book from such a broad assortment, then grabbed hold of the wheeled ladder with both hands and dashed madly across the room, trundling it in front of her. When the ladder reached top speed, she promptly jumped aboard and began climbing. Her plan was to wait until she had come to a stop, whereupon she would simply pick the first book she saw in front of her. It was a good plan, and would have worked well, too, if the ladder had not hit a sticky spot just as it was slowing down, catching her in an awkward position and depositing her unceremoniously on the hardwood floor.

When Maxine opened her eyes, she found herself staring up at the ceiling, stunned but unhurt. She turned her head a bit and saw that she had dislodged a single volume, which was lying now in front of her nose. Kipling's *Plain*

Tales from the Hills. She dusted herself off and collected the old book, retreating from the shelves to find a spot where she could curl up to read.

The far side of the library was all windows, which would have made it a cheerful room if the rain had not still been pelting down steadily outside. A leather chair was turned toward a cold hearth and grate, and Maxine flopped down here with her legs slung over one arm and her head on the other. For a while she labored over her book, but it had already been too long a day for stories of British soldiering. Her thoughts drifted off—back to her little black terrier, Baron, who would have been on the chair beside her if she were home; back to her mother's face, pale and gaunt the morning Maxine had boarded the train out of Chicago.

She turned to the window and watched the raindrops, beading and running, wandering aimlessly down the glass like the drowsy visions in her head.

CHAPTER 2

The doorbell chimed, waking Maxine with a start. She heard noises in the entry hall—the front door opening and closing and then a shout.

"Ahoy! Anybody home?"

Maxine sat up straight in her chair and rubbed her eyes. "In here," she called tentatively.

A moment later the double doors to the library burst open with a bang.

"Hello," said a boy who looked to be close to her own age. "I figured you must have shown up already. The cabdriver told me this was his second trip out here today."

He was as thin as a soda straw, with blond hair and enthusiastic blue eyes, and short trousers that showed a pair of skinned knees.

"Do you remember me?" he asked, shaking himself like a waterlogged dog.

"Not really," said Maxine, which was mostly the truth, though she knew perfectly well whom she was looking at.

"That's okay. You're Max, right?"

"Maxine," she replied coolly.

"I'm your cousin William," said the boy. "William Battersea. Your family came down from Chicago to visit us in Kansas City a few years ago. You had less freckles back then, though." He squinted at her closely. "Maybe they're multiplying," he added with concern.

Maxine struggled mightily to resist the urge to look at the end of her nose. She considered her freckles to be impolite material for conversation. Not that she was particularly concerned with her cousin's opinion of her looks, of course. Generally speaking, when she glanced in the mirror, the girl she saw staring back struck her as perfectly ordinary— shoulder-length brown hair, brown eyes, limbs and features all roughly where they were expected to be. Nothing to make babies cry or cause pedestrians to cross the street shuddering, certainly, just nothing likely to make anyone notice at all. Except the freckles. People always mentioned her freckles, as if they were the most important thing about her. It was a tiresome topic she had come to despise, and as a result, she had taken to wearing the color red as a kind of misdirection—a single scarlet embellishment on any given day, like the silk ribbon she wore now in her hair. Something that stood out. Something impossible to ignore.

She was about to say a word or two about the rudeness of commenting on other people's appearances, but William was already galloping on.

"It's a swell old house, isn't it?" he said, craning his neck to take in the expansive library.

"I guess so," she replied. "It's certainly . . . big."

"Yeah, and mysterious, too. Think of the fun we'll have this summer exploring all the dark corners and secret rooms."

Maxine frowned with disapproval. "I'm sure we don't have permission to go poking around in every—"

"Say, you don't suppose this old place is full of hants, do you?" interrupted William.

"Hants?"

"You know, spooks, ghosts, murdered people whose souls can have no rest and all that."

"I think that's perfectly morbid," she said, and she was on the verge of changing the subject when William beat her to it.

"Have you seen Grandpa yet?" he asked.

She shook her head.

"Really?" said William. "How about a housekeeper or butler or something?"

"Nope. I just let myself in."

"That's a little funny, don't you think?" said William, scratching an eyebrow. "I hope Grandpa's all right. I mean, I hope he's not soft in the head, as long as we're stuck with him for the summer and all. My folks seemed sort of worried about packing me off to stay here while they were travel- ing. Mom says he was always a strange old bird, even before Grandma died."

Maxine was lost in reflection for a moment, trying to

recapture something from the past. "He used to bounce me on his knee when I was little and pretend I was riding Man o' War in the Derby. It made me laugh—" She stopped short. She hadn't meant to say the words aloud, and she glanced at William, expecting to catch him sniggering at her, but he only nodded in a thoroughly genuine sort of way.

"You still remember all that?"

"Not exactly," she said, cocking her head self-consciously. "It's a story I heard from my father. I can't really even picture what Grandpa looks like."

"It's kind of odd, isn't it?" said William. "Meeting your grandpa for the first time, like a perfect stranger?"

"I don't know," Maxine replied. "No odder than meeting your own cousin, I guess."

Which is how William Battersea and Maxine Campbell made each other's acquaintance on a rainy day in New Jersey in 1929. Because they shared the same grandfather and had both just finished the seventh grade, they might have expected to have a fair amount in common. But as the conversation rambled on, they began to suspect that their respective apples had fallen on opposite sides of the Battersea family tree and had apparently rolled down the hill into entirely different counties.

"You know, if we're going to be here all summer," said William at length, "we probably ought to come up with some nicknames for each other."

"Nicknames?" replied Maxine, using the most patient tone she could manage.

"Sure. Something I can call you that's short for Maxine."

"I guess I didn't realize it needed shortening."

"You don't care much for Max, right?" he said, squinting at her like an artist studying a bowl of fruit. "How about I call you M? Like the letter, you know?"

"If you must," she said tartly. "If you think Maxine is likely to overtax your brain."

William stared at the ceiling, contemplating the daunting prospect of using multiple syllables to address his cousin for the whole summer.

"Well," he said, "if you don't like it, maybe we could think of something else. What do they call you at school?"

"Who?"

"I don't know, teachers, classmates . . . *friends* . . ."

Maxine ignored the question and turned toward the window.

"You have friends, right?" he asked.

"Sure," she said, watching the rain patter on the trees outside. "I'm absolutely rolling in them. I mean, does it really matter?"

"Personally, I wouldn't have any use for school if I didn't have friends there."

Maxine glanced at William, wondering if he expected a response. "The truth is," she said at last, "the kids at school aren't much interested in me, and I'm not much interested in them. And what difference does it make anyway? The boys are all oafs, and the girls are a pack of silly geese."

"Well, that pretty much covers everyone," said William with a smirk, "but at least nobody can accuse you of playing favorites." He paused. "You know what you are? You're a mis—a misslethroat!" he said, snapping his fingers.

"A what?"

"You know, a sourpuss, a—a mankind hater."

"It's *misanthrope*, dumbbell, and no I'm not. It's just that I think they're all so childish. I watch their playground games and their popularity contests, and the whole thing makes me yawn. There must be about a million ways I'd rather spend my time."

"Such as?"

"Such as anything. Making real decisions. Meeting important people. Whatever it is grown-ups do."

"Oh, I see. You want to be grown-up," said William with a serious nod. "What's your big hurry?"

"For one thing," Maxine said, "when you're an adult, people ask your opinion. And when you give it, they listen."

"People don't care about your opinions?"

Maxine snorted delicately.

"Not even your family?"

"I'm the baby," she said. "Nobody cares what the baby thinks. My sister, Anne, spends her life in front of the bathroom mirror, and Remy's off to college in the fall and everyone acts like he wrote the book. And ever since my mom got sick, Dad's been too busy fussing over her to pay any attention to me. My mother was the only one who ever really thought I was worth listening to."

William cocked his head and bent at the waist to meet her downward gaze. "I think you're worth listening to, M."

Maxine raised her eyes from the floor and glanced at him to see if he was serious.

"And as near as I can tell," he added playfully, "you're already grown-up."

Maxine managed a dour smile and paused to look her cousin over more carefully. He gave the distinct impression of a puppy in the park—tail wagging constantly, nose poking under every unexplored stone, eyes always watching for a game or a tease. The general effect was a pleasant one.

"So if we're going to have nicknames," she said, "I guess I'll have to start calling you Will."

"Naw, dumbbell is fine, thanks," he replied, and he gave her arm a pinch.

CHAPTER 3

Outside, the dreary day had surrendered feebly to night, and the windows in the library turned to dark mirrors. William had prowled off in hopes of finding some clue to Grandpa's whereabouts and maybe something to eat as well, leaving Maxine to potter listlessly about the empty room.

Her eye landed on the spine of a thick, leather-bound book lying on the mantel above the fireplace, and she mounted the hearth for a closer look at the gilt cover—a beautiful maiden kneeling on a silk cushion before the throne of a brooding sultan—but the pages inside were covered in strange, swooping characters, and she could make no sense of them. She closed the book in disappointment and was just stepping down from the hearth when she noticed a curious symbol carved on the front of the stone mantelpiece: a solitary zero inscribed within an embellished medallion—the identical twin of the emblem she had seen above the doorbell.

"Wadja lookigat?" said an unintelligible voice by her ear.

Maxine jumped. Behind her, William's greasy lips and bulging cheeks hovered over her shoulder. "I found something to eat," he said with a hard swallow, raising a half-gnawed turkey leg.

"So I see," said Maxine with a look of thinly veiled disgust. "Do you want to make yourself sick? That's probably spoiled, you know."

"The ice in the icebox hasn't all melted, so it can't be over three or four days old."

"Three or four days? How long has Grandpa been gone, anyhow?" fretted Maxine. "I mean, honestly, Will, there must be some mistake. Maybe he forgot we were coming."

"Aw, you worry too much," he said. "Have a bite of turkey."

Maxine frowned and pushed his hand away.

"Do you think he even wants us here?" she asked.

"What do you mean?"

"I mean, when our parents asked Grandpa if he would take us for the summer, well, he really couldn't say no, could he? Not with my mom being so sick and all . . ."

William wiped his mouth with the back of his sleeve. "I thought it was Grandpa who suggested the whole thing."

"Really?" she said. "Why would he? He's never shown any interest in us before."

"No, I guess he hasn't," said William.

"So what are we supposed to do now? Clean out his icebox, sit in his easy chair, go upstairs and find a bed? It's like 'Goldilocks and the Three Bears.'"

William snorted, but his attention had drifted to something else.

"Hold this," he said, handing her his turkey leg.

"What are you doing?" asked Maxine. She watched as he tugged on one of the blackened andirons in the fireplace.

"Looking for the hidden lever," he said, scanning the room. "The entrance to the secret room is almost always in the library. All you have to do is find the lever." He braced himself against a section of the bookshelves and put his back into it, but the shelves refused to budge.

"You've been spending too much time at the movies," said Maxine. "This is just a disagreeable old house. We're more likely to die of boredom this summer than anything else."

"Says you. Old places like this always have a trapdoor or an underground passageway—someplace where Grandpa keeps his pirate treasure and dead bodies."

He pulled hard on a brass candleholder attached to the wall, and it came off in his hands with a shower of crumbling plaster.

"Will! What on earth? Are you trying to get us in trouble our first night here?"

William shrugged and tucked the candleholder behind the drapes. "Maybe it's not in the library after all. Let's go check the rest of the house."

He rattled out of the library and down the main hall, tapping on every knothole and peering behind every picture frame along the way. Maxine sighed and followed along half-heartedly. They paused at the old grandfather clock, but just as William began to open the glass case, the doorbell rang.

The cousins both turned sharply and stared at the front door.

"Maybe it's Grandpa," whispered Maxine.

"Why would he have to ring his own doorbell?" replied William, and without giving his cousin a chance to reply, he trotted to the door and opened it wide.

A dark, rawboned man stood on the front step. He wore plus fours and high boots, and his beard was long and matted. His eyes darted furtively as he scanned the moonlit drive, and then he turned to face the open door. Seeing the children, he frowned with dismay.

"I was expecting Colonel Battersea," he said.

"Can we help you, mister?" asked William.

The man made a circle with his thumb and forefinger and held it to his chest, watching the children for a response. Maxine and William stared back blankly.

The stranger's brow knit with concern, and he glanced back over both his shoulders. "I have a telegram," he said, his voice low. "It's vital that this reach him." He handed them a sealed envelope. "You'll make sure he gets it?"

"Of course," said Maxine. "May I tell him whom it's from?" She blinked at him expectantly, but the man turned without a word and hurried down the steps.

"Well, that was odd," said Maxine. She closed the door and glanced at the envelope, then leaned it against Caesar's bust on the pedestal beside the staircase. "He seemed awful jumpy about something, didn't he?"

"Say what?" mumbled William, looking the old clock up and down again, as if he had forgotten the strange visitor entirely.

Maxine groaned. "You're still thinking about your secret door, aren't you?" she said.

"Notice anything unusual?" he asked, rapping on the sides of the case.

"Besides the fact that it's the biggest clock I've ever seen? No."

The clock really was gigantic. It was taller than a grown man and as wide as a cart horse.

"Look behind it," he said.

"I can't," she replied as she walked around it. "There's no gap. It's sort of . . . attached to the wall."

"There's something else," he said, pressing his ear to the cabinet. "Have a look at the side table."

She glanced at the table beside the clock. An empty vase and a black telephone flanked an old Royal typewriter. In front of it, a silver letter opener stood fixed in a block of cork. Maxine wiggled the blade free and tested the point with her finger.

"Is it Grandpa's murder weapon, do you think?" she said,

holding it delicately between her thumb and forefinger with a look of mock horror.

"Very funny. I mean the typewriter. Why would he keep it in the front hallway? Shouldn't it be in the study or something? And why is there a wire coming out of it?"

Maxine bent and looked under the table. A cord snaked down the table leg from the back of the typewriter and disappeared into the wall beside the clock.

"It's weird, isn't it?" said William. "Like maybe the typewriter can send out some kind of electrical signal."

Maxine frowned skeptically, but William stepped up to the typewriter and cracked his knuckles like a piano maestro.

"O-P-E-N S-E-S-A-M-E," he muttered as the ebony keys clattered beneath his fingers. He stopped and stared at the grandfather clock expectantly, but nothing happened.

"B-A-T-T-E-R-S-E-A," he said, trying again.

The clock seemed indifferent to his advances, and William's brow twisted in frustration, but he continued to peck away with admirable tenacity.

"Knock yourself out," said Maxine. "There's nothing here. No revolving bookshelves or scandalous letters or bodies stuffed in the walls." She turned away and had just made up her mind to wander back to the library when she froze in her tracks. Her gaze had landed on a familiar symbol engraved on the letter opener in her hand—the same strange symbol she had seen on the doorbell and the mantelpiece. Her eyes narrowed, and she turned back toward the clock.

"Slide over," she said with a nudge. William obliged,

retreating to the blue mosaic fountain, where he sat down on the lip of the stone basin beneath his cousin's hanging coat. Maxine squinted at the typewriter, shook her head, and pressed the number zero.

From somewhere inside the walls, the cousins heard the faint squeal of metal on metal.

The skin on Maxine's arms prickled like a cucumber, and her eyes shot to the tall case beside the stairs, but the old clock's even tick continued without pause.

Then, from a spot just above William's head, there came a mechanical clunk.

He raised his eyes slowly and craned his neck backward until he was looking at the coat hooks directly above him. While he watched, the blue mosaic swung inward on unseen hinges.

"A door," he whispered.

Indeed, a yawning portal now loomed inside the stone archway. Steep steps tumbled down into the darkness below. Maxine and William stared at each other in amazement.

Suddenly, Battersea Manor seemed much less boring.

CHAPTER 4

"We're not going in there," Maxine said, peering down the darkened staircase. "I mean, we should probably wait for Grandpa, don't you think?"

But the seductive voice of Adventure was already crooning softly in William's ear, drowning out Maxine's misgivings.

"What do we need Grandpa for?" he replied. "Permission? If he were really all that worried about us getting into trouble, maybe he should have been here to keep us out of it."

Summoning his courage and taking his cousin firmly by the arm, William led the way through the secret door.

The stairs creaked beneath them as they descended, their hands and feet groping blindly in the gloom. Maxine's resolve grew weaker with each step downward, but she tried to reassure herself by glancing back to the top of the stairs and the thin shaft of light beyond the door.

Presently the stairs ended, and the cousins perceived that they were in a sort of musty, narrow passageway. William shuffled on, but Maxine faltered at the thought of leaving behind the light at the top of the stairs.

"Will, let's go back," she begged. "Please?" And then, in the same breath, she let out a scream.

"What's the big idea?" yelped William.

"Sorry. Something brushed my face. I think it was a cobweb."

William waved his hand nervously in her direction.

"I just felt it, too," he said. "It's a string or something."

He gave it a pull, and the passage filled with light. They squinted in the sudden brightness. When their eyes adjusted, they found that they were in a low passageway constructed of rough stone, empty except for a bare lightbulb above and a red door at the far end. The door was unmarked, save for an ornate zero that embellished the brass doorknob.

William and Maxine looked at each other with puzzled expressions. And then, without pausing long enough to change their minds, they crept toward the door, turned the knob, and stepped across the threshold.

The smells and textures were what captured Maxine first. The fragrance of incense combined with the somewhat less pleasant chemical undertone of formaldehyde. Heavy velvet curtains framed the inside of the doorway they had passed through, and to their left, a pair of leather chairs, cracked and burnished from years of use, faced each other on a threadbare Persian rug.

William brushed past Maxine into the dim room, his face bathed in the eerie green glow of a murky glass tank that stood behind the old club chairs. As he approached, the water within stirred, and in the haze he perceived the slow movement of a dozen silvery piranhas, each profile showing a single cold eye and a sullen, malevolent underbite of razor-sharp teeth.

Behind him, Maxine flipped a switch beside the door, lighting the entire room. William's gaze drifted up the facing wall, pausing on a battered wooden propeller flanked by an assortment of harpoons and brightly feathered blowguns. A pith helmet sat atop a penny arcade shooting gallery, along with a set of rusty thumbscrews and a drugstore candy jar full of gleaming glass eyes, which stared, unblinking, in a hundred different directions. Exotic hunting trophies glowered down from the walls above—rhinos and Cape buffalo and an assortment of predatory cats, their jaws forever frozen in a succession of indignant snarls.

The collection lined the shelves, hung from the ceiling, and crowded every corner. Dusty maps, pagan idols, and aboriginal boomerangs; glass jars with pickled biological specimens floating gray and limp in a chemical brine; signal kites and hubble-bubbles and tarnished helmets—and none of it inside a glass case or behind a velvet rope but everything right out in the open to pick up and examine. Suffice it to say, the basement was like nothing they had ever seen before, and indeed, like nothing in the rest of stuffy old Battersea Manor.

"Have you ever seen so many amazing things in one place?" said William, stooping to examine a collection of iridescent blue butterflies and the stone bust of a handsome Egyptian princess.

Maxine shook her head and turned in a slow circle, gaping at the hoard of oddities that surrounded her. It was a stupendous collection, promising hours of wide-eyed discoveries. But more compelling yet, to Maxine's way of thinking, were the long rows of photographs that covered the walls—an enticing arrangement of windows to adventures past and parts unknown—and she studied each of them with fascination.

Many of the pictures were of a young man who must have been Grandpa, taken in some exotic locale, sometimes with a woman Maxine assumed was her grandmother, but more often with a group of dusty legionnaires or painted natives. In one, Grandpa's left arm was bandaged and hung lamely in a sling, but his right arm still shouldered his rifle, and before him lay the limp form of a lifeless panther. In another, Grandma sat perched on his shoulders with a panicky expression while he waded across a wide stream, laughing devilishly at her predicament.

They looked happy in the photos, hand in hand, young and strong. He was handsome and tall, with a wide, easy smile beneath a sweeping mustache—his eyes creased with a perpetual squint earned on cloudless plateaus and a thousand safaris. She seemed graceful and sturdy, in love and untouchable, like a woman who laughs at the future. In every picture her hair was piled in a stylish chignon, though inevitably a few unruly strands managed to escape, falling into her eyes and giving her a careless appearance. Maxine suddenly felt a throbbing ache at the thought that she would never have the chance to know her. She touched her grandmother's face, then sighed and turned away.

William, meanwhile, had just backed into a spherical object suspended from the ceiling. The thing was slightly larger than a baseball—withered and coffee-brown, like a spoiled apple hung in his cellar back home. It swung gently from a long tangle of black hair. He gave it a poke, and the wrinkled lump twisted slowly in the air until he found himself nose to nose with a tiny misshapen face.

William worked down a dry swallow. The eyes and mouth were stitched shut, and a bit of bone pierced the nostrils, and although the skull had been removed and the blackened features were grisly and deformed, there was no question that it had once been human.

"Ugh," said Maxine, walking over with her nose wrinkled in disgust. "Grandpa's sure got some strange ideas when it comes to decorating."

William prodded one of the stitched eyelids. "What? You mean you don't have shrunken heads dangling from your ceiling back home?"

"Will," she said, "do you think he's—do you think he's *normal?*"

"Normal?" he replied. "Do you mean ordinary? No, I think we can safely say our grandfather is far from ordinary."

"But do you think he's—"

"Bats? Off his rocker? It's possible. He sure does collect some strange toys."

Maxine shuddered. "I don't know if I can stay here all summer with a crazy old geezer."

"So maybe he's got a loose screw or two," said William. "What's the difference? The way I figure it, we're old enough to take care of ourselves."

"That's an earful, coming from someone who can't even match his own socks," said Maxine, pointing at his ankles and rolling her eyes. "Listen, Will, we have no idea if we can trust him. As a matter of fact, we don't know the first thing about him. What if he really is crazy? Or worse?"

William frowned. "Aw, go on," he said with a wave. "Next you'll be telling stories about the bogeyman. It'll all be all right. You'll see."

The cousins soon lost all track of time in the bowels of the cluttered basement. The trail of curiosities led them farther on and deeper in, until at last they reached the remotest corner of the long room and found themselves at the foot of an enormous wooden crate.

"Hmm," murmured William. "What's this?"

The pine box stood on end, its hinged front nailed shut, giving it an allure similar to the famous chest that Pandora opened once upon a time, with such dire results. And one detail in particular was impossible to ignore: in shape, the crate was very like a coffin. As the cousins' eyes met, there was no doubt that they shared the same impression.

"What's Grandpa got in there?" asked William uneasily.

The lid was pasted with several shipping labels and a conspicuous yellowed tag, which Maxine dusted off with her shirtsleeve.

"*Noli me tangere*," she read.

"Is that Greek?" asked William.

"Latin, I think," she replied. "I've seen it before, in a book at school."

"What does it mean?"

Maxine traced the words with her finger, racking her brain, and the translation came to her suddenly from the depths of memory.

" 'Touch me not.' "

CHAPTER 5

William scuttled away, leaving Maxine alone with the crate for several uncomfortable moments before reappearing with a rusty claw hammer he had scrounged from an old toolbox.

"What do you think you're doing?" Maxine asked suspiciously.

William flashed her a devious grin, brandishing the hammer as he approached the wooden crate.

"Oh no you don't," she said. "We are *not* opening up that box, Will."

"What an interesting suggestion," he said innocently. "To be honest, the thought never even crossed my mind—but now that you mention it, count me in."

"Do you need your head examined?" she chirped. "The label says hands off."

"Don't worry. If Grandpa asks whose idea it was, I'll be sure to give you all the credit."

"Oooh," said Maxine, grinding her teeth in aggravation. "I could just pinch you to death!"

"Oh, come on, M, don't be such a cold fish. Aren't you even a little bit curious to know what Grandpa's hiding in there?"

Maxine folded her arms across her chest and thought for a moment. "I guess I am," she said finally. "Maybe I need my head examined, too."

William started near the bottom, wedging the claw end of the hammer under the lid. He pried, and the first nail made an evil screech the cousins felt in the roots of their teeth. As the crack yawned, a shiny black centipede writhed out of the gap, and William recoiled with revulsion.

"A stowaway," he said, wiping his hands on his shirt before returning uneasily to his task.

He worked his way up the lid, standing on a footstool to reach the final nail, which proved more stubborn than the rest. Maxine felt sure that he was about to pull the whole box down on top of them with a great crash, when suddenly the nail gave way, the lid sprang open, and William tumbled off the stool, bowling his cousin over in the process. The smell of mildewed packing straw filled the room.

William and Maxine caught their breath and scrabbled backward on the floor.

Towering over them was an ominous figure—eight feet tall at least—a colossal wooden statue stained as black as darkest midnight and polished to a gleaming luster. It was clad only in a crimson loincloth that brushed the floor between its widespread feet, and a spherical glass vial was slung round its neck on a thick gold chain.

The figure's sinewed shoulders and powerful haunches seemed to knot with menacing intent, and an evil-looking beard of braided horsehair hung down over the naked chest. But far and away the most disturbing aspect of the whole spectacle was the countenance that leered at them. Between a broad, flat nose and brutal brow, two deep-set eyes of black glass glittered wickedly and fixed the cousins with a malignant stare. The jaw was hinged, and the mouth hung open in an obscene gape, which conjured up the uncanny impression of a great black serpent prepared to swallow some enormous prey.

"Wh-what is it?" whispered Maxine.

William didn't answer but crawled forward on hands and knees to retrieve an old envelope that had fallen from the open crate. Keeping a nervous eye on the wooden statue, he unfolded a yellowed letter and read the contents.

My dear Colonel Battersea,

It was immensely gratifying to receive your inquiry. As a professor of Near Eastern history and a collector of rare antiquities, I was fascinated to hear of the artifact you have in your possession, and hope that I may be able to shed some light on its substance and essence.

Your wooden figure is highly unusual, but it is not unknown in this corner of the world. To put it plainly, it is a vessel of sorts—a supernatural receptacle for a being known as the jinni.

The jinni, as I'm sure you are aware, is without physical body. The jinn are believed to be creatures of purest fire, and no mortal can lay hold of them, any more than a man may grasp a twisting flame. But the old legends say that in dark corners of the world, in dark times, men sought out forbidden knowledge and found the means to trick the jinn and capture them in lamps or flasks, like the one worn around the neck of your carved figure.

In the end, though, these sorcerers realized that a bottled jinni was of no more use to them than a liberated one, and so in order to bend them to their purposes, they fashioned wooden statues—vehicles for the jinni's smokeless fire—and they called these figures al-kaljin, or "spirit steeds." Animated by the spirits of the jinn, the wooden marionettes were roused to stalk the world of men.

A word or two about the particulars of the process are probably in order. To breathe life into the wooden colossus, the glass flask containing the jinni's imprisoned spirit is placed inside the open mouth, and in due course an abraxas, or an abracadabra, as you would call it, is spoken aloud. The precise words, in this case, are "Rise and obey," and when the command is uttered, the dark eyes of the al-kaljin will flicker, the rigid limbs will turn supple, and dead wood will rise, compelled to do the master's bidding.

There is more that could be said, of course, about the origins of the al-kaljin and the secrets of the jinn. I have never had the opportunity to put the lore to the test myself, but if you happen to attempt awakening the creature, please send word, as I would be most interested to learn of the results.

Until that time, I remain, indubitably,
Your humble servant,
Baltasar Anawi, PhD
University of Damascus

William folded the letter and scratched his forehead thoughtfully with his hammer.

"A jinni," murmured Maxine, approaching the wooden figure and tapping the glass flask with her finger.

"So," asked William, "are you game?"

"Game for what?"

"Waking it up, of course. What else?"

Maxine's face clouded.

"I mean, we wouldn't actually make it do much," said William. "Have it turn around and touch its nose . . . ask it to say its name. Maybe we could get it to dance the Charleston."

"Can it grant wishes, do you think?" asked Maxine.

"I expect. Every self-respecting jinni I've ever heard of can grant wishes."

Maxine's thoughts flitted to her sick mother.

"All right," she said. "Do it quick, before I change my mind."

William obliged, mounting the stool again to stand face to face with the creature. He grasped the vial and prodded it delicately into the figure's yawning maw as if he were feeding a goldfish to a moray eel.

"Now we're on the trolley," he muttered, descending from the stool and taking a large step backward. He cleared his throat nervously and pointed at the creature.

"Er . . . *Rise*," he said. *"Rise and obey."*

The figure showed no sign of life. It stood silent and still, with never so much as a twitch.

"Maybe try and sort of . . . close the mouth a bit," Maxine suggested.

William raised his eyebrows at Maxine's recklessness with *his* fingers, but he gave it a decent effort, gingerly forcing the heavy jaw up until it closed partially on the vial.

"Rise and obey!" he said again, louder this time. He pulled away and watched the figure closely for a moment.

"Aw, this thing is a big hoax," he said with disappointment. He shrugged at Maxine and turned his back on the crate.

At that moment they were startled by a noise upstairs. Heavy footsteps crossed the floor above them. A voice called out.

"Grandpa!" said William. "He's home!"

Maxine blinked at him in a panic.

"We shouldn't be down here, Will!" she cried. "We shouldn't have opened the box!"

William slammed the lid of the crate and tacked it shut with a single nail. Tripping over the clutter in the basement, the cousins scrambled for the stairs.

CHAPTER 6

Maxine and William slunk from the darkened stairway and found the entry hall unoccupied. Breathing a sigh of relief, they pulled the secret door shut behind them and tiptoed toward the library.

"Good evening," said a voice above them.

The cousins both jumped like tripped mousetraps, and their eyes shot to a tall, gray-haired gentleman descending the stairs.

"I didn't startle you, I hope," said Colonel Battersea in a plummy British accent. "I was just looking for you in the upper halls." If he knew of their visit to the basement, he showed no sign of it.

"Welcome to Battersea Manor," he said. "Maxine, I presume. And this must be William."

The cousins weren't certain whether he expected a hug

or a salute, but the old colonel settled the matter by offering an outstretched hand.

"Where've you been?" asked William. "We thought you'd forgotten all about us."

"Eh? Forgot about you?" replied Grandpa. "Oh yes, yes of course. My apologies. I had every intention of being here upon your arrival, but I've had a bit of urgent business to attend to, and I've only just now returned."

Grandpa's face was lined with years, and his handlebar mustache was gray now, but his eyes still glinted with the vitality of the man in the photographs downstairs. His features might have been carved from flint; taken in total, they hinted at an intimidating intellect. He leaned against the banister and loosened his tie, then gave a long sigh. His mind seemed elsewhere.

"You look a bit bedraggled," he said, coming back to himself. "Are you hungry? The housekeeper won't return until tomorrow morning, but I imagine we can rummage up something in the pantry."

He led the way into the kitchen, and the cousins sat down at a small table near the window and watched him boil water for tea. They waited in silence for an uncomfortable length of time, but Grandpa's face was brooding, and he offered no conversation.

"What's this?" asked William, pointing to a photograph on the wall of a younger Colonel Battersea and his wife standing atop the Great Pyramid of Giza. "It looks like it was taken in Egypt or something. Were you some sort professional adventurer? Like Lawrence of Arabia or Richard Halliburton?"

"Dick Halliburton," Grandpa scoffed. "Hmmph! Dandified travel writer. No, no, that was hardly my style. I've had my share of adventures, all right, but I never sought them out for their own sake." He stopped and frowned. "Haven't your parents told you anything about me?"

"Not really," William said.

"No," muttered Grandpa. "I expect not."

"They said you traveled a lot, and that you worked for the British government," Maxine chimed in.

"Ah, that much is true. Although your grandmother was an American and we made our home here, I am a British subject. I've worn many hats over the years—done some soldiering, some amateur mapmaking, a bit of diplomacy. And I've been a great many places, I suppose. Traveled Asia, Africa, and the Continent, spent a time in South America. I ended up in the Levant—or the Near East, as they're calling it now—and that was where I stayed for the remaining years of my service to the Crown."

"And Grandma came along?" asked Maxine. "She followed you to all those places?"

"Your grandmother traveled with me as often as it was possible, at least until the children—your parents—were born. And there were long stretches when I was home with her as well."

Maxine's thoughts drifted back to the pictures in the basement. "Do you miss her?" she asked.

Colonel Battersea poured the tea as if he'd never heard

the question, then turned and considered his granddaughter carefully.

"How are things at home, young lady? How is your mother?"

Maxine was silent for a moment.

"She coughs," she said in a hollow voice. "She coughs and she can't stop, and her face is as white as chalk, and she can hardly breathe. And sometimes when it's over, there's blood on the pillow."

Grandpa cleared his throat. "Yes, well, we can certainly hope her trip abroad will do her some good, can't we?" he said, arranging a trio of scones and a dish of clotted cream on a tray. "She'll be staying at the best hospital in Europe, after all."

Maxine's eyes dropped, and she twiddled with the buttons on her sleeve.

"So, Grandpa," said William, breaking the awkward silence, "what exactly did you do for the British government all those years?"

"Hmmm, what indeed. You aren't the first person to ask that question, of course. But perhaps I should save a few of my secrets for another day. For the time being, let us just say that I protected His Majesty's interests wherever I was needed."

Grandpa placed the tea tray on the kitchen table and sat down beside the children.

"And now," he said, "I want to hear about yourselves. Details, mind you. I'm anxious to know what sort of a hand I've been dealt."

The cousins squirmed for a moment under his intense gaze, then proceeded to struggle through a fractured account of hobbies and classmates and music lessons while Grandpa listened and nodded at regular intervals.

"Very interesting, I'm sure," he said at last. "But tell me, now that you have spent some time together here at Battersea Manor, you must be getting to know each other a bit, eh? I am eager to learn a little of what you have discovered. Above all else, I would like to hear what redeeming qualities you have found in each other—what is it that you most admire?"

It was an odd question, and the cousins traded uncomfortable glances.

William pondered for a moment. "Mostly I'd say Maxine is smart. A sharp tack. She's read all kinds of books, and she's good at figuring things out."

"Ah, intelligence. A fine trait. Yes. And, Maxine, what about William?"

"I think Will's very brave," she said. "I'm a great big chicken, but he's not afraid of anything."

"Bravery, eh? How do you know?"

Maxine's immediate thoughts were of the expedition to the basement and William's insistence on opening the pine box, though mentioning these details to Grandpa would hardly do.

"I'm not sure," she said. "He's got a lot of nerve, I guess. He's already explored just about every dark corner of this house."

"I see. Yes, well, you've made fair judgments, given that

you've known each other only a very short time. But I must say, I believe you are both quite wrong. These are not your worthiest attributes. There are greater gifts in heaven and on earth. When the summer is over, perhaps you will have a very different answer."

The cousins fidgeted restlessly and tried to vindicate themselves with an intelligent response, but found themselves at a loss for words.

"Well, that's enough lecturing for one night, I suppose," said Grandpa. "Perhaps it is time to turn in. Let me show you to your rooms."

CHAPTER 7

In the middle of the night, Maxine woke to the wind moaning outside her window. Her bedroom was on the third floor of the manor, and the treetops groped at the pane. But it was something else that had stirred her from sleep.

"M!" whispered a voice outside her door.

"Will? Is that you?"

"Yeah. Are you awake?"

"No," she said.

The door creaked open, and William slipped through.

"What are you doing sneaking around in the dark?" asked Maxine.

"Nothing." William shrugged. "I just couldn't sleep. I can't get my mind off the jinni. When I lay my head on the pillow, I still see those glittering eyes and that grinning mouth."

"Just be glad it never came to life," said Maxine, taking some comfort in the fact that her cousin had not escaped their adventure entirely unscathed.

"You don't want to go down and try again, do you?" William asked.

Maxine sat up in her bed. "In the middle of the night? No thanks. We shouldn't have been in there in the first place," she said. "I'm sure Grandpa must have seen us come up through the secret door."

"Aw, so what? Don't you think maybe he *wanted* us to find the basement? That it was all just part of the test?"

"What test?" she said. "There is no test."

"Oh no? What was the little interrogation in the kitchen all about, then? Grandpa's trying to measure our character, see what we're made of."

"That's silly, Will. You're inventing things."

"Maybe. He didn't exactly welcome us with hugs and kisses, though, did he? One thing's for sure—he's not the sort of granddad who sings you to sleep in his rocking chair. He'd rather meet you with blades at dawn, if you know what I mean. Lunge, parry, feint—that's what it's like talking to Grandpa."

Maxine pondered this, watching the shadows of the tree limbs braid across the moonlit floor, but her thoughts were interrupted by a creak in the hallway outside.

"Did you hear something?" she whispered, listening carefully. The corridor was quiet now.

"Must've been a hant," said William. He turned out the

lamp on the night table and made a low groaning sound that rose and fell in a tortured wail.

"Stop that," said Maxine, groping for him in the dark and tossing a pillow in his direction.

"I told you this place was haunted," he said with a wicked chuckle.

"Let me go to sleep, would you?"

"All right, I'm leaving."

He tiptoed to the door.

"Good night, Will," said Maxine.

"Good night, M," said William, and the door clicked shut behind him.

Maxine's eyes opened to dawn's pale light seeping through her dormer window. An elusive dream lingered in her mind, but try as she might, she couldn't bring it back. She crawled from her bed, following a strange urge.

The house was still, and she padded barefoot down the hallway, past the uneven snores in William's bedroom. Climbing a flight of stairs at the back of the house, she found herself in an unfamiliar corridor. The rooms here had undoubtedly belonged to the Battersea children once upon a time, wallpapered with faded barnyard animals and circus tents, all empty apart from a few forgotten pieces of shrouded furniture that had been pushed to darkened corners. Pictures and toys and books were gone. An eerie, unnatural witching hung over the space. Maxine began to feel a desperate need to uncover some trace of the living—something that proved her mother had been here once, that she had known this place.

At the end of the hall Maxine found the nursery. The room was sad and dreary, full of echoes. An empty crib stood against the wall beside a dusty, half-draped wardrobe. She approached the wardrobe uncertainly, as if it were a giant jack-in-the-box, and, pushing aside the dingy sheet, she threw it open. There was nothing inside.

Sighing, she glanced across the room at a colorfully painted door, and even though every other closet on the floor had been a disappointment, she decided she would check it all the same. The knob yielded to a halfhearted tug, and the door swung wide.

Maxine let out a gasp.

Here at last she had discovered the resting place of her mother's childhood. Small coats and dresses hung neatly above worn black boots. Sagging shelves held dolls and hoops and balls and bats. The air smelled of mothballs and old leather. Maxine burrowed among the hanging garments, feeling them all around her on her arms and face. She pushed through to the cool smoothness of the back wall, then turned around and slid to the floor, where she sat and peered out from behind the clothes.

The faint toll of church bells echoed somewhere far off, and she listened, sitting perfectly still like the china dolls beside her. She touched the cherub lips of the closest one and wondered where her mother might be now. On the deck of a ship, maybe, taking the sun, recovering her strength and thinking of Maxine.

Her eye flitted absently around the closet, and something peculiar stirred her from her daydreams: a pair of names had been scratched on the inside of the doorframe.

Helen and Eddie

Helen was her mother, and Eddie—that was Will's father, her uncle Edward.

Beneath these, she found a strange scrawl:

Keep the secret, never tell,
unless you want your throat to swell.

Her fingers trembled as they traced the words. She pictured her mother and uncle crouched inside the closet, sharing some concealed confidence. She wondered how long the words had rested there in the dark, unread and unspoken, hidden from every human eye until this very moment.

There was something else. A photograph had been tucked into the baseboard: a faded picture of a teenage boy standing with a suitcase on the front steps of Battersea Manor, and on the back a single letter and a date:

D—June 1909.

"Who could this be?" she wondered aloud.

Downstairs, the old grandfather clock chimed the half

hour, calling Maxine back to the present. She yawned and thought of her soft pillow and warm bed, but as she stood to go a battered milliner's box on the shelf caught her eye. Inside she found a lovely red hat that smelled faintly of perfume, and though it had no tag or monogram, the old felt cloche was pierced by a long hat pin set with a bright ruby— her mother's birthstone.

The hat fit perfectly. She tucked the strange photo under the inner band and, clutching her new treasure to her chest, Maxine crept back to her bed.

Later that morning the cousins stumbled down into the kitchen, rubbing sleep from their eyes. A small, matronly woman stood at the stove stirring a bubbling pot, her steel-gray hair pulled back in a fist-sized bun of formidable tautness and immaculate symmetry. Colonel Battersea was already at the kitchen table, going through a stack of mail.

"Good morning, William, Maxine," he said. "Though it seems you've managed to sleep most of the morning away. I don't suppose you drink coffee? No, your parents are more responsible than that, I'll wager. All the same, it looks like you could use it, eh?"

William mumbled something incoherent and flumped down at the table.

"Ah, bad dreams, perhaps. Well, no matter, you're young and resilient. Mrs. Otto, don't you have any oatmeal for these children?"

Mrs. Otto shot him a withering look. "Give me half a moment, won't you? They've only just come down." She ladled out the oatmeal and slid a bowl in front of each of the cousins while the old colonel opened another letter from the stack in front of him.

"By the way," said Maxine offhandedly, tilting a pitcher of milk over her bowl, "a telegram came for you yesterday."

Grandpa's face darkened abruptly, and he pushed aside the post.

"Is that so," he said. He slid back his chair and rose to his feet, leaning over her. "And when were you planning to mention this?"

"I don't know," replied Maxine, glancing nervously at William. "Just now, I guess. I kind of forgot about it."

"Well?" he said sharply. "Let's have it, then."

Maxine hurried out to the entry hall and returned with the envelope, handing it contritely to her grandfather, who tore it open straightaway and immersed himself in the contents.

Mrs. Otto cleared the pots from the stove and put them in the sink. "All right, Colonel, I'm off to see my sister, like I told you last week," she said. "I won't be back until tomorrow afternoon."

Grandpa grunted but didn't look up from his letter, and Mrs. Otto shook her head at him and untied her apron. "I've put the groceries in the pantry and left a smoked ham in the icebox," she said. "You'll have to fend for yourselves this evening." And she marched off with no further farewell, leaving them alone in the kitchen.

Grandpa turned his back on William and Maxine and reread the telegram, muttering to himself as if the words were all gibberish, but his concentration was broken by the jangling ring of the telephone in the entry hall. Crumpling the telegram and tossing it on the breakfast table, he disappeared from the room.

"Nice going, M," said William. "Why didn't you give him the telegram last night? He doesn't seem real happy about it."

Maxine glared at him through slitted eyes. She raised her spoon, letting her oatmeal slowly dribble back into her bowl, and was about to offer a scathing critique of William's own significant shortcomings when they heard Grandpa's startled voice in the hallway.

"What? Are you sure? But when?"

The cousins got up and edged close to the doorway and found that if they held their breath and strained their ears, Grandpa's words were faintly audible.

"So they are here, then, on our own shores. The long arm grows longer still. . . .

"No, no, the timing of your call is more than mere coincidence, it seems. I received a second telegram just this morning. It mentioned a courier—I believe a certain package is to be delivered into my possession. . . .

"That much is difficult to say. The telegram was vague on several points. The time was clear enough, but I'm unsure of the location."

His voice dropped, and the cousins could no longer make out the words.

"What's Grandpa up to?" whispered William.

"I don't know," answered Maxine, "but it doesn't exactly sound like he's retired, does it?"

"No, not so much," said William. His eyes darted to the telegram in the middle of the table, and he crept toward it, his hand outstretched.

"We shouldn't, Will," said Maxine. Her voice lacked conviction, though, and she crowded close to him and peered over his shoulder as he unwadded the crumpled sheet and smoothed it carefully on the table.

```
        IMPERIAL AND INTERNATIONAL
          COMMUNICATIONS LIMITED
               "Via Eastern"


  Iskenderun, Turkey

  May 20, 1929

  =COL H BATTERSEA C/O REG OFF BROOKLYN =

  THE JACKAL HAS FLUSHED THE FOWL.

  COURIER RUNNING. WHEN THE HARE GROWS FAT

  SEEK THE NEEDLE FIND THE EYE.

                  - YUSUF
```

"It's like some kind of riddle," whispered William. "Does any of that make sense to you?"

Out in the entry hall, the telephone receiver rattled in its perch.

"Will, he's coming back!"

William crumpled the paper again, dropping it onto the table like a hot biscuit just as Grandpa rounded the corner.

The colonel's face was troubled.

"Something has come up, I'm afraid," he said. "There's a matter I must attend to in the city. I'll be gone for a day or two."

"You're leaving us alone again?" cried Maxine.

Grandpa rubbed his knuckles. "No, not alone. Your parents would never let me hear the end of that," he muttered. "You can stay here with Mrs. Otto. Now where has she gotten off to?"

"She said she was going to her sister's house, remember? She said she'd be back tomorrow afternoon."

"Blast. I can never count on that woman for anything," fumed Grandpa.

He looked at the cousins with irritation.

"I'll have to take you with me, I suppose. Go get yourselves ready."

"What, now?" Maxine blurted out.

"Yes, now. When else?" he said, checking the weather outside the kitchen window. "Pack your things, and see if you can find an umbrella while you're at it. We have a train to catch."

CHAPTER 8

Upstairs in the colonel's bedroom, Grandpa and William packed an old leather suitcase, while Maxine searched for an umbrella among the cupboards and chests of the mansion's upper halls. Umbrellas were in short supply at Battersea Manor, it seemed, and in the end she settled for her mother's red hat—not exactly what Grandpa had in mind in terms of rain gear, perhaps, but just the thing a sophisticated young lady would wear on a trip into the city. She clapped it on her head and bounded down the stairs.

Tumbling into the entry hall, Maxine was surprised to find the front door slightly ajar. She gave it a puzzled look and pulled it shut, but she suddenly felt a disturbing tingle at the nape of her neck and let out a sharp gasp. She was not alone in the front hall. Two strangers stood behind her, pressed flat against the staircase. They wore coveralls and long black coats, with heavy boots and short-billed caps, and one of them carried a pair of hooked ice tongs across his shoulder. As she turned, both of them reached for something inside their long coats.

"H-hello?" said Maxine warily. "Are you here to deliver the ice?"

The men's vigilance relaxed when they saw her face, and their hands returned to their sides.

"Where is Colonel Battersea?" asked the man with the iron tongs, his words laced with a peculiar accent.

Something about the men chilled Maxine to the bone. They had dark complexions and hungry eyes, and they moved stealthily, licking their lips as if they could taste her fear.

"He's upstairs somewhere," said Maxine, growing more alarmed by the second. "He'll—he'll be down any minute."

She opened her mouth to call for Grandpa, but the man lunged at her, clamping his hand over her mouth like a pipe wrench. Maxine's eyes bulged above his fingers. The man said nothing but forced her gaze to meet his.

The second man inspected the room calmly, methodically. He rapped on the blue tiles of the fountain and opened the case of the old clock, then brushed his fingers across the keys of the typewriter and disappeared into the kitchen.

The man who held Maxine looked down into her eyes with a soulless stare. He tilted her head sideways and scrutinized her profile, then shook his head indifferently.

His confederate returned from the kitchen waving a wrinkled slip of paper that Maxine recognized straightaway as Grandpa's telegram, and the two men exchanged words in a foreign tongue.

There was a noise from above—footsteps on the stairs. The intruders glanced at each other and pushed Maxine aside, and then, as if they shared a single mind, they sloped toward the door. At the threshold the hindmost stopped and turned, producing a silver coin from his pocket.

"Give Colonel Battersea our regards," he said, tossing it at her feet.

The door slammed shut behind him, and Maxine sank to the floor and sobbed.

Grandpa's voice drifted down from upstairs. "Coats and hats, both of you. It may be chilly this evening in the city," he called. He carried his leather suitcase and was pulling on a pair of driving gloves as he descended, but when he saw Maxine, he took the last few steps two at a time and crouched at her side.

"Are you hurt?" he asked, helping her to her feet.

She shook her head slowly.

"What happened?" asked William, pelting down behind.

"They took it," choked Maxine. "They took the telegram."

"Who? Who took the telegram?"

"There were two of them, dressed like icemen. They had strange accents."

Grandpa peered out the window and opened the front door, but they were gone. The muscles in his jaw knotted, and he turned his attention to the grandfather clock. Opening the case, he stopped the pendulum and slid back an interior panel behind the counterweights to reveal a small brass knob. With a twist and a heave, the clock released from the wall and trundled out into the middle of the room like a prodigious drawer, pulling behind it a glass display case fully ten feet in length.

"I knew that old clock was hiding something," breathed William. He pressed his nose to the glass and gaped like a fish. The top shelf of the display case was lined with a long column of sinister daggers—black-hilted, razor sharp— each one glinting like a silver thorn. The bottom shelves housed an arsenal of pistols and scatterguns and a handful of grapefruit-sized clay spheres of indeterminate purpose.

"What's with all the knives?" William asked.

"Hmm . . . ," replied Grandpa distractedly, "trophies, I suppose." He opened the case and selected a worn Webley revolver, and the cousins watched with morbid fascination as he checked the cylinder and holstered it under his coat.

"And these funny little clay pots?" asked William, plucking one from the case and tossing it casually in his hand.

Grandpa caught the sphere in midair and gave him a reproachful look. "Perhaps it's better not to touch, my boy. The grenadoes contain Greek fire—a combustible concoction that explodes when the shells are shattered, igniting an inferno of startling proportions."

He turned the clay sphere over twice in his hands, checking it with care, and then replaced it gently.

Maxine, understandably, had lost her train of thought for the moment, but it returned to her presently. "The men who took the telegram—they left you this," she said, holding out the silver coin.

William took it from her and raised it to catch the light. "It looks old," he said.

"A Persian obolus," said Grandpa without even glancing up.

"Is it supposed to mean something?" asked William, pocketing it.

The colonel nodded. "It's a threat of sorts," he said. "The coin is meant to be placed in the mouth of a corpse, to pay the ferryman for passage to the shores of the dead."

CHAPTER 9

The sun was high in the sky as the train left Hendon and rattled north into the countryside. Maxine and William sat across from Grandpa, faces drawn as they stared out the window. The wheels on the tracks beneath them clattered and whined as a series of telephone poles whisked by endlessly, almost imperceptibly, so that the passing world seemed to dance on the glass like a shimmering projection.

The opening scenes were sleepy and rural. Scissor-tailed swallows swerved through impossible arcs in the warm, angular rays of early afternoon, Guernseys grazed contentedly on tufted green hills, hay barns freckled the fields, and an occasional horse cart rolled along beside a muddy canal. Gradually, farms gave way to houses, dirt tracks to streets; church steeples pierced the horizon, and bicyclists paused at intersections, watching the train rumble by. Neighborhoods blossomed, Main Streets swept past, and row houses stretched back from the tracks in long queues, dotted with women on stoops and children playing ball in the street.

"Grandpa," said William, watching the scenery flit past, "what's going on? Why do you have to go into New York City?"

The colonel stirred as if he'd been called back from someplace far away. "I have an appointment to keep," he said. "It's nothing you need worry about."

"Does it have something to do with your old job in the British government?"

Grandpa sat up straighter, eyeing the other passengers on the train cautiously. "Trust me, my boy," he said in a low voice, "the less you know about my affairs, the better. I'm bringing you along only because leaving you home alone was not an option. Indeed, it now appears that Battersea Manor is no longer safe."

"What did those men want with Maxine?" William asked.

"It wasn't Maxine they were after," replied Grandpa. "It's with me they have a score to settle. It seems they were rather keen to learn the contents of my telegram."

"I don't understand," said Maxine. "Why is that telegram so important?"

"Egads," said Grandpa. "Is there no end to your questions?"

Maxine tried to mask a hurt look. "We were only curious," she said.

"Yes, well, curiosity has a habit of killing the cat, the saying goes," replied Grandpa. "Not to mention larger, two-legged animals from time to time."

The cousins shifted uncomfortably in their seats.

"Perhaps I'm overstating my case," said Grandpa with a conciliatory wave. "After all, you seem to have survived your expedition into the Adventurers' Club with no serious side effects."

"The Adventurers' Club?" asked William tensely.

"Yes, yes, of course—the room you found in the basement."

The cousins' cheeks flushed scarlet.

"Come now"—Grandpa chuckled—"you look as if I'd caught you with your hands in the biscuit tin. You didn't really think I was ignorant of your little escapade, did you?" He leaned in close and tapped his nose conspiratorially. "It was fortuitous, really. An opportunity for me to see what the two of you are made of."

"So the whole thing *was* a test!" growled Maxine, folding her arms over her chest.

Grandpa frowned at her. "Don't be cross, my dear," he said. "Life is full of tests. And in this particular case, you proved yourselves magnificently. Your discovery of the secret door and your efforts to animate the jinni were quite impressive."

"But how did you know?"

"When I arrived home, the door to the basement was ajar. I may have heard a thing or two."

"We couldn't wake it up," William said. "The magic words didn't work."

"No, of course not," replied Grandpa. "Fortunately for you, my jinni speaks Arabic. It doesn't understand English, be it the Queen's or your tragic American variation."

Maxine's brows lowered skeptically. "You mean it's all true? That stuff we read in the letter about bringing the jinni to life?"

"Ah, now that's a dodgy business, trying to rouse a jinni," said Grandpa with a wink. He paused for a moment, and the twinkle in his eye dimmed, as if Maxine's question had called to mind some other, darker matter.

"Perhaps—perhaps I should tell you a story," he said. "As I recall, your parents were rather partial to my bedtime stories."

He cleared his throat and motioned for them to sit back in their seats.

"Long ago and far away," he said, "there lived a crafty old jinni—"

"The same one you've got in your basement?" asked William.

"No, no, of course not," said Grandpa impatiently. "Now sit quietly and listen.

"On a rocky crag in the middle of the desert, the jinni built a mighty fortress, and there inside the soaring parapets he sat and nursed a lust for power and conquest. He could not accomplish his ambitions alone, he realized, so he gathered about him a host of servants—a veritable army, raised from the desert sands.

"The jinni was full of dodges and deceptions and dia-bolical tricks of every sort, but he had one trick in particu-lar that trumped all others. Within his secret chambers he kept a mirror. This mirror was believed to have certain magi-cal properties. It was said that in it the jinni could see all things—things past, things yet to come, and things that were far away. And by the glamour and sway of the magic mirror, he compelled his servants to carry out his every command.

"With the help of the mirror, the old jinni's power swelled, and in time it came to pass that all the desert lands around him fell under his hand. Yet even this was not enough, and his aims grew bolder still, and in the end he set his mind to conquering the whole world.

"His grand scheme met with an obstacle along the way, however. While his attention was focused on the far reaches of his empire, an unexpected threat found him—a threat much closer to home. One day while his back was turned, a desert fox crept into the jinni's fortress, and she stole the magic mirror.

"He cursed and raved, the old jinni, and his power was shaken. He did his best to conceal the loss of his prize from his servants, but all the while he was searching, hunting far and wide for the fox, hoping to recover what was stolen and to take his revenge."

Grandpa produced a silver pocket watch from inside his gray suit coat. He opened it and stared at something on the inside of the case, lost in thought.

"He never found her," he said at last. "And he never found the magic mirror."

The cousins squinted at him expectantly.

"Is that it?" asked Maxine. "Is that how the story ends?"

But Grandpa didn't answer. He closed his watch again, and he suddenly looked old and tired.

"So I thought," he murmured. "Perhaps I was wrong."

The old colonel fell silent and turned toward the window, and presently his narrative was eclipsed by the drama outside as the row houses along the tracks shouldered skyward. Snug bungalows were replaced by tall storefronts and then again by still taller tenement buildings draped with laundry that waved as they passed. In the streets below, automobiles honked at traffic lights, streetcars squealed on their winding rails, and young men idled under streetlamps, until at last the train plunged into the North River Tunnel and emerged with a great rush on the east banks of the Hudson in a thunderous finale of steel spires and mighty stone towers.

The train rolled on through the long gray canyons and pulled into Penn Station with a slow, grinding stop. The passengers collected their parcels, a sleeping sailor across the aisle yawned and rubbed his forearms, and the doors opened onto the rumbling city.

"Here you are," said Grandpa, slipping William a dollar bill. "Some folding money in case the two of you get hungry later. Don't flash it around."

They stepped down from the train into the crush of passengers that trudged along the platform. The cousins paused and turned in place two or three times in an attempt to get their bearings, but they would have had better luck trying to hold their ground in the middle of a swift river—a far less hostile place, in truth, than where they stood now.

"Swell view, eh, kid?" said a barrel-chested man, shouldering William aside with a passing glare.

Lingering was obviously impossible, and they fell in step behind Grandpa, who pressed ahead with fixed purpose.

"Where are we headed?" William called out.

"The Algonquin Hotel," said Grandpa over his shoulder. "We'll check in and get you situated for the evening. Once the two of you are both asleep, I must leave the hotel for an hour or two."

"In the middle of the night?" said Maxine.

Grandpa nodded. "My rendezvous is at midnight," he said, "under the Hare Moon."

"The Hare Moon?"

"You've heard of the Harvest Moon? It's the name given to Luna in the month of October. But other months have different names. Now we are in the moon of May—the month the Indians called the Milk Moon. In China it is known as the Moon of the Dragon. But back in England my grandfather always called it by its old European name—the Hare. It was almost full last night, and tonight it will be in all its glory."

" 'When the hare grows fat . . . ,' " muttered William, repeating the lines from the telegram.

"What's that, my boy?" Grandpa called back.

"Oh, nothing," said William, and he trotted to catch up.

They had just reached the end of the platform, where the plodding procession slowed at the foot of the cast-iron staircase that led to the overlooking concourse, when the man in front of them dropped his traveling bag. The case burst open, spilling out a heap of papers at his feet. The man sank to one knee and fumbled for the loose leaves, bringing Grandpa and the children to a standstill, along with everyone behind them. William bent to help, but the colonel pulled his grandson firmly to his feet. His eyes darted warily from side to side, and his hand groped inside his coat.

Behind them, a square-jawed stranger in a dark suit caught Colonel Battersea's arm, pinning it to his side. In the same instant the bumbling man at their feet abandoned his scattered papers and rounded on them. Grandpa aimed a kick at the man's head, but the attacker arched like an eel, and the boot only grazed his temple. With a furious rush he took the colonel by the lapels and drove him backward into the crowd, bowling William and Maxine to the ground as he went. Grandpa shouted something to them as the two men carted him off, but the words were swallowed up by the whistle of a locomotive on the next track that shuddered to life with a thudding jolt and a heavy squeal.

A blast of steam engulfed the platform, and the cousins struggled to their feet, whirling frantically, squinting for a glimpse of Grandpa's silver hair or his battered leather suitcase. The engine churned out of the station, the seething vapor dissolved, and William and Maxine found themselves alone amid a spreading drift of trampled papers. They dashed up and down the platform in a panic, but it was in vain.

Colonel Battersea had vanished.

CHAPTER 10

The cousins staggered up the stairs toward the concourse in a daze. A railroad policeman stood at the railing above them. Spotting his navy-blue uniform and gold badge from a distance, Maxine and William snapped to life and barreled up to him.

"Officer, come quick!" said William, tugging at his sleeve. "It's an emergency!"

"Beat it, you two," he said with irritation.

"Honest, sir!" cried Maxine. "Somebody just kidnapped our granddad!"

"I've been standing here for an hour, kid. I never saw a thing."

"But he was right down there! I'm telling you, Officer, you couldn't miss it!"

"And I'm telling *you* it never happened," said the cop,

swinging his billy club indifferently on a loop around his finger. He bent over them and scowled.

The cousins slumped in bewilderment, realizing that any slim hope of rescuing Grandpa was slipping away by the minute. They launched into another round of appeals, but the officer waved his hand.

"Listen, you got a problem, go file a report. Stationmaster's office is by the central entrance."

Pelting away, they traversed the main concourse, a monumental cathedral of glass and steel that vibrated like a great beehive, swirling with shopping bags and felt fedoras and steel-toed boots. They wormed their way through the crush, invisible beneath the sea of adults that surrounded them, and managed to reach a small window on the far side of the great hall with a sign above it that indicated they had found the stationmaster's office.

"We just lost our grandfather," panted Maxine through a round hole in the window.

"Somebody grabbed him," William added.

A whiskered woman in brown flannel stared at them through thick spectacles.

"End of the line," she said.

They stared at her with confusion.

"There's a line here. You'll have to wait your turn."

The cousins glanced behind them and saw a long queue. Deflated, they circled to the back and waited helplessly as the line inched forward at a snail's pace.

They reached the window at last, and the woman in

brown looked up at them, her jaw slack and her glasses reflecting a vacant light.

"We lost someone," William said.

"Lost and found is at the other end of the station," droned the woman, turning her attention to the next person in line.

"Not something . . . *someone*."

"You're lost?"

"No, we're not lost, but our granddad is."

"Your grandfather is lost?" said the woman impatiently.

"Sort of. I mean, somebody kidnapped him."

The woman's eyes narrowed, and she peered at William.

"Well, I don't know if you'd call it kidnapping exactly," he said. "He's a grown man. But two fellas grabbed him."

"If there's been a kidnapping, why, that's something for the railroad police."

"But it was the police who sent us here!" protested Maxine.

The woman let out a martyred sigh and handed them a clipboard and a pencil. "You'll need to fill out this report before we can make any calls. Take a seat."

The cousins sank down against the base of one of the soaring steel pylons that supported the concourse ceiling. William licked the tip of his pencil and did his best to make sense of the endless rows of blanks. A thousand faces swept past, checking watches, toting packages, tramping through the station without offering them so much as a glance.

Maxine's thoughts slipped back to her last glimpse of Grandpa, and she put her hand on her cousin's arm.

"Do you think he's all right?" she murmured.

"Grandpa? Sure he's all right," William said unconvincingly. "I guess he probably pinned those fellas' ears back and tied them up with their own shoelaces."

Maxine tried to smile, but she couldn't wink at the memory of the two men.

"Say, were those the same two who stole the telegram?" asked William.

She shook her head. "I'm not sure. I don't think so."

"They looked like city types," he said. "Tough guys, you know?"

He realized Maxine was watching him closely, and he pushed down his own lingering doubts.

"Don't be such a worrywart," he said, knuckling her in the ribs. "We'll hand in this report if it will make you feel any better, but Grandpa will turn up before you know it. Just you wait and see."

But Grandpa did not. Afternoon drifted into evening with all the urgency of a thistledown on a sultry summer day, and in the meantime the cousins sat in glum silence, waiting for the stationmaster's office to bring some word of Colonel Battersea.

"Maybe we should try to find Grandpa ourselves," said William at last.

"Are you kidding?" replied Maxine. "In New York City? It'd be like trying to find a needle in a haystack."

William grunted and rose to stretch his legs. He wandered along the edge of the concourse, pausing to look at a row of travel posters along the wall. THE BROOKLYN BRIDGE . . . TIMES SQUARE . . . CARNEGIE HALL . . .

All at once he felt Maxine behind him.

"Look at that one," she said, pointing at the last poster in the row.

The picture showed a tall stone obelisk atop a grassy hill. Their gaze dropped to the lettering at the bottom:

CLEOPATRA'S NEEDLE—CENTRAL PARK

"What about it?" William asked.

"I think maybe we just sat on the needle in the haystack, that's what," she replied. "The telegram—it mentioned a needle, remember?"

"'Seek the Needle, find the Eye . . . ,'" he murmured, and suddenly his eyes widened. "M, you're a genius!"

"Is this what the telegram was talking about?" she asked.

"It has to be! We already know the when, right? Grandpa said the meeting would happen at midnight tonight—when the Hare Moon grows fat. This poster must be the where. How far is Central Park anyways?"

"I'm not sure," said Maxine, grabbing a map of the city from a nearby tourist kiosk. She unfolded it and studied the contents for a moment. "Two or three miles, I guess."

"It's time for us to go," William said.

Maxine's eyes narrowed. "What are you talking about?"

"Sitting around here is for the birds," he said, glancing

at a clock above the office window. "We're wasting our time. We've only got a few hours until midnight. If we don't go now, we'll miss Grandpa's appointment."

"Grandpa's appointment—without Grandpa?" she said. "You can't be serious!"

William stared up at the cat's cradle of steel trusses and arched glass high above, trying to form the currents inside of him into words.

"Remember yesterday at Battersea Manor," he said, "when you told me you were tired of your classmates and all their silly games—that you wanted to do something grown-up? Well, here's our chance."

"Not now," Maxine insisted. "Grandpa could be here any minute."

"We can do this, M. Meeting the courier was the whole reason Grandpa came here. If it was important enough for him to risk bringing us along, then it's important enough for us to go on without him."

Maxine sighed, too tired to argue. "Okay, so we're going out in the dark, to find a stranger and collect a package in the middle of Central Park." She looked hard at William, measuring his confidence, wondering if it was enough for both of them.

"Sure," he replied. "If you can get us there."

CHAPTER 11

A ragged breeze swept down Seventh Avenue as they passed through Penn Station's towering granite columns into the open street. There in the shadow of the city, the two cousins craned their necks to take in the noisy universe that towered above them.

This was Empire. Glamour and vice and movie-house newsreels come to life, a world of ticker-tape parades and red carpets, gin mills and Tommy guns. An empire, by all counts, too busy to acknowledge a young boy and girl lost in the evening rush. Taxicabs honked impatiently in the street and paperboys hawked late editions as William and Maxine tramped north beneath the steel frames of rising skyscrapers whose bones knit under the welding torches and rivet hammers of an army working high above the earth.

William glanced sideways at Maxine as they walked. Her face was cramped in a look of singular determination.

"You scared at all?" he asked.

"I don't know," she said. "I've had so many scares in the last couple of days, I think maybe I'm starting to build up an immunity."

William nodded. "Are you sure you know where we're going?" he asked.

"Sure I'm sure," replied Maxine, glancing twice from her map to the corner signpost. "The park's straight north from here." She wrinkled her nose and gazed down Thirty-Third Street like a sibyl searching the stars.

In the meantime, William's attention was drawn to a small crowd gathered beneath the elevated tracks. At the center of the cluster he found a man with a greasy collar seated atop an overturned bucket. On a crate in front of him were three walnut shells—or half shells, to be exact—and he turned them over in succession to show that one concealed a pale green marble. Covering it again, he proceeded to shuffle the shells in a dizzying weave.

"Where's it at, kid?" he asked coolly, lifting his hands from the crate.

William looked over both shoulders and realized that the question was meant for him. He pointed to where he thought the marble was hidden. The man flipped the shell and there, gleaming like a burnished emerald, sat the green marble. William smiled in spite of himself, surprised at how easily he had seen through the man's sleight of hand.

"Say, that was pretty nifty," said a lanky stranger in the crowd.

"Eight bits says you can't do it again," sniffed the man on the bucket, rearranging the shells.

"Aww, applesauce," said the stranger. "You show him, kid."

William grinned, warming to his audience and swaggering a bit in the spotlight. He saw clearly where the marble came to rest . . . fairly clearly, at least . . . and he motioned to his choice, but the man clucked his tongue.

"Let's see the cabbage, runt."

William's hand went to his pocket, fingering his train ticket and a box of safety matches and the old Persian coin, and then he found Grandpa's dollar bill and laid it on the crate. The man on the bucket nodded and turned over the shell, but the marble was gone.

"Tough luck, champ," said one of the crowd. "You'll get 'im next time."

The shells danced on the crate again, and the man looked at him expectantly.

A knot twisted in William's stomach, and he stood in stunned silence, feeling like an ear of shucked corn. His fingers twiddled with the old silver coin in his pocket, and he had a desperate thought that perhaps the man would play him for it, but then he felt a tug at his arm. Maxine shook her head infinitesimally and nudged him away from the crate.

"Gee whiz, kid," said the thimblerigger, "you ain't gonna let Dumb Dora here call the shots, are you?"

The group around the crate laughed broadly and slapped William on the back. The jeers punctured William's freshly swollen ego, and his face burned hot. He tried to back out of the crowd but stumbled over his own feet. Maxine caught him by the shoulder, and they retreated from the circle, sniggers and catcalls following them as they left.

"Never mind them, Will," she whispered, feeling a bit bruised herself.

He didn't answer, only stared straight ahead and quickened his stride, leaving her a step behind.

"What were you thinking, anyway? That was all the money we had," she said. "You know it was a swindle, right? He wasn't going to let you—"

William's face went rigid, and Maxine abandoned the lecture. She fell in step beside him without another word, and they both walked on, pilgrims in an unknown land.

It was late when William and Maxine reached the bright lights of Fifty-Second Street. Evening had settled on the city, and the inhabitants of twilight—the nighthawks and the drugstore cowboys, the pearl-strung flappers and the Brylcreem dandies—all began to slink from their dark corners to swim in the warm current of night. Up the block, the silky notes of a cornet wafted from a jazz club, and winking bulbs chased themselves silly around a corner marquee.

The cousins arrived at Central Park as the full moon was climbing over the trees. Carbon-arc lamps flickered to life along the sidewalk as they ventured off the street into an entrance along the park's southern edge. A leafy tunnel of branches arched overhead, marking the boundary of a world of organic shapes and sounds that seemed not to belong among the smooth, concrete surfaces of the city.

Entering the park felt like crossing over into a dream, as if they had entered the forest of a fairy tale, and as a matter of course, dark and ominous events must presently commence. Here at the threshold they glanced about meekly, but the park, it seemed, was vacant and still. The even clop and steady creak of a plodding horse and carriage was audible through the trees; the cousins listened until it finally moved on, then shuffled forward down the overhung path that lay before them.

They soon realized that, despite the quiet of nightfall, the park was not entirely deserted. A gentleman out for his evening constitutional gave them a nasty start, passing them from behind and excusing himself as he disappeared down the path. Other souls remained, couples mostly, lingering on park benches, sitting so close they were a single silhouette. William and Maxine hurried past, their eyes fixed resolutely ahead. They kept their conversation to a whisper without knowing why and quickened their pace between the scant pools of light cast by the streetlamps.

Over the crest of a small hill, the path turned and ran under one of the arched tunnels set beneath East Drive. They both cringed at the sight of the black, sepulchral opening.

"What are we doing here?" Maxine asked, her words echoing hollowly inside the stone passage.

"In this tunnel, you mean?" asked William.

"This tunnel, this park, this city . . . I mean, doesn't it seem like we're flirting with disaster?"

"Flirting?" replied William. "I'd say we've leapt right into her arms, more like. Try not to think about it." He turned up his collar and quickened his step. "Hurry up, or we'll miss the courier. It must be nearly midnight."

They had almost reached the end of the passage and were just beginning to breathe easier when they had the sudden realization that they were not alone. Another presence was there with them in the darkness—motionless, silent—standing close enough to reach out and throttle them both, watching them wolfishly. The murk of the tunnel was so impenetrable they had almost passed the man without noticing him, but now he inhaled on a thin black cigar and the orange glow reflected faintly in his hooded eyes. A current of terror coursed through them, and they shied like startled antelopes and bolted down the path.

The man watched them go and sauntered out of the tunnel, disappearing among the trees.

CHAPTER 12

Atop a wooded hillock, in a lonely corner of Central Park, lies a wide, cobbled circle. Within this ring, at the very center, stands Cleopatra's Needle, a gift from the viceroy of Egypt to the citizens of New York in 1880. It is a striking geometry, six feet wide at the base and all of seventy feet high. William and Maxine were still panting as they climbed the stone steps and saw the Needle through an arch of cedars, illuminated dramatically from below and rising like a spire into the night sky. The reflected light cast a wide halo on the ground around the ancient obelisk, a dwindling pool of luminescence bounded by trees and bushes. Above, the Hare Moon hung high in the sky, lending its own cool radiance to the scene.

At the edge of the ring they crouched in a clump of brush that offered some degree of cover from passersby. A small opening in the foliage provided a clear view of the

Needle, and they peered out, cheek to cheek, like hedgehogs in a burrow. Elbowing aside a tangle of twigs and leaves, Maxine produced two ham sandwiches wrapped in wax paper from her coat pocket.

"Where'd you get those?" asked William.

"The kitchen. I made them before we left," she replied, passing him one of the sandwiches.

"You don't happen to have a cherry pie tucked under that old red hat of yours, do you?"

"No, but I've got a chocolate bar here somewhere," she said, chewing lickcrishly as she peeked out through their leafy porthole. "Who was that in the tunnel, do you think?"

"Beats me," said William. "The Grim Reaper, probably."

He was quiet for a moment, the wheels turning in his head.

"Here's a real question for you," he said. "Which do you think would be better—falling to your death or being buried alive?"

Maxine looked at him as if he had a wet, drippy cold and had just sneezed on her.

"Or being bitten by a deadly poisonous snake?" he added as an afterthought.

"Which would be *better?*"

"Yeah, I mean, I was just looking at the Needle, thinking about how tall it is and what a mess it would make if you took a swan dive from up there, and that reminded me of the guys who built it—the Egyptian pharaohs—burying their servants alive in the pyramids, and then I thought of Cleopatra and how she got bitten by some kind of viper or asp or something, and I was just wondering to myself, which one of those would be the best way to go?"

"Maybe we shouldn't talk," said Maxine.

"I guess getting buried alive would be best," William continued. "I don't love snakes, and heights make my legs feel like jelly. Climbing trees is all right, though. I don't know why. Maybe because you've got branches below you and you can't—"

"Did you see something move over there?" Maxine asked sharply.

"Where?"

"In the bushes across the way."

"I didn't see anything."

They fell silent, watching and listening.

"Will! Look! Someone's there, on the far side of the circle! Let's try and get a better look."

She was just about to crawl out from their hiding place when a tall figure stepped into the light not more than twenty feet away.

Maxine stifled a gasp, and William pulled her back by her coat. Peering through the hedge, they watched the man stop directly before them, with his back turned. He was silhouetted against the orange glow of the obelisk, and smoke curled around his head as he scanned the circle. He turned slowly, and they recognized his smoldering cigarillo. He wore a wine-red fez of stamped velvet, and in the pale moonlight they could make out a sable mustache and a shining, greased goatee that tapered to a curling point.

His clothing was unremarkable in most respects, similar

to what any tailored gentleman might wear about town—white shirt, pressed trousers, and boots—but he was clad in an unusual knee-length black coat with a high collar and no clasps, and on his hand he wore a thick silver ring.

"Is that the courier?" whispered William.

Maxine shook her head with horrified certainty.

A twig cracked beneath William, and the tall man stopped dead, his gaze boring into the foliage. The cousins held their breath and watched as he swayed slightly, his face calm and composed. Both of his arms hung slack. He dropped his cigar and crushed it beneath his heel, then crept toward them, massaging his temple with his ring finger.

A high, warbling trill sounded from the far side of the circle. The man's head jerked round. He turned on his heel and strode away.

The cousins exhaled aloud and sagged weakly with relief. They struggled to their feet and stretched their frozen joints, and had just begun to clamber from the bushes when a pair of hands seized them from behind with an iron grip.

CHAPTER 13

"Get down!" hissed a voice.

The unseen stranger yanked them back into their hiding place, where the cousins lay motionless, petrified with fright.

"Who are you?" gasped William.

"Where is Colonel Battersea?" came the reply.

The timbre of the voice startled William as much as Grandpa's name.

"It's just a kid," he whispered. "A girl!"

"I am meeting Horatius Battersea here tonight," said the girl, speaking the words with a careful accent that leaned hard on every syllable. "Where is he?"

"Are you the courier?" asked Maxine.

"I came with a package," said the girl. "I seek Colonel Battersea's protection. My name is Nura."

The three children scrambled out of the brush and retreated from the Needle, staying in the shadows and off the paths.

"The man at the obelisk—who was he?" asked William, breathing hard.

"He belongs to the Hashashin," answered Nura. "They are the enemy—the servants of the Old Man of the Mountain."

The cousins' faces were blank.

"The Old Man is the author of bloodshed," said Nura, "the king of all the sons of pride. His eye and his blade reach everywhere."

She walked quickly and offered no further explanation, leading them down a wide gully that wound through a thick stand of elms. They emerged in a remote quarter of the park, behind a small, shingled pavilion, and there, in the light of a solitary streetlamp, the cousins finally came face to face with their new companion.

The girl's skin was the color of oiled teak; her lashes were long and thick, her teeth uneven but pearly white. She wore a checked shawl over her smooth dark hair, and a coarse brown dress that brushed the ground. Across her shoulder she carried a canvas haversack. Her face was solemn, and although she was slight and seemed rather breakable, she set her jaw and met their eyes directly.

"Where are you from?" asked William.

"How'd you find us?" Maxine added.

"Do you have the package?" they both said at once.

Nura only shook her head at them and asked, "Where is Colonel Battersea?"

"Not here," replied Maxine coolly. "He sent Will and me."

The two girls eyed each other with suspicion.

"You can trust us—honest," said William. "Colonel Battersea is our granddad."

At this Nura's brows lifted slightly.

"If you give us the package, we can take it to him for you," William added.

"You're the courier, right?" said Maxine, watching the tight-lipped girl carefully. "You *do* have a package for us?"

Nura's defiance faltered, and she looked away. "I had it," she replied. "The parcel was lost."

"You mean you lost it. How clever of you." It was a petty, mean-spirited thing to say, but Maxine couldn't help herself.

"I carried the parcel safely for six thousand miles," said Nura with a glare, "on horseback and on foot, by camel and by ship. No harm came to it. Only here at the end of my journey was it snatched from my hand." She turned away to hide the tears welling in her eyes.

"Aw, don't pay any attention to Maxine," said William. "She's pretty much a world champion when it comes to making people feel small."

He thought for a moment. "How old are you, anyways?" he asked.

"Twelve."

"And you traveled six thousand miles to get here?" he said with a low whistle. "So what happened? With the package, I mean."

Nura shut her mouth and said nothing, but the cousins' stares were so steady and expectant that finally she shook her head and sighed.

"A month ago I left my home in Turkey with the parcel," she said.

"Were you alone?"

"Who sent you?"

Nura halted and gave them a stinging look that made it clear she would suffer no further interruptions.

"I left home and traveled the desert road over many hills and plains and came to the coast, to the house of a friend of my father's. I rested there, and then the man put me on a ship bound for America. For two weeks I never left my berth, except for necessities. I made myself *gorunmeyen*—invisible. The package I kept with me always, as I was afraid for it, and there was no knowing which of the passengers might be the enemy. For the length of the voyage I spoke to no one.

"Then, two days ago, I arrived here in New York and met disaster. I left the ship. There were long lines, hundreds of people, men asking questions and stamping papers. When it was all over, my feet and my head ached, and I sat down on a bench to rest. My long journey had left me weary, and I was careless.

"The package was in a leather satchel that I carried over my shoulder. I took it off and placed it by my side. A man sat down next to me on the bench. He wore a white hat and white clothes that were not fitting, and I didn't care to look at him—he was like a sneaking animal. But for some reason, I don't know why, I only pulled the bag closer to me and closed my eyes to rest. That was my ruin."

Nura's voice cracked, and she paused, resenting the memory.

"The man tore the bag from my arms and ran down the street, clutching his hat to his head. I was crying out, 'Stop!' but the people all around just moved out of his way, staring like sheep."

"Was he the enemy?" asked William. "Hashashin?"

Nura shook her head impatiently. "Impossible. He was clumsy and stupid—a common thief."

"So why didn't you go to the police?" William asked.

"I found a policeman, yes." Nura nodded. "He laughed and told me to forget the package. He said it was hopeless. He said I would never see my bag or the thief again."

"Well, of course not," replied Maxine. "The police aren't going to search the whole city for one bag belonging to a little gir—"

"But I *did* see the thief again," interrupted Nura, and her eyes flashed. "I went back this morning to the place where the bag was taken. He was wandering the harbor in the same white suit and hat, like a rat scratching in his favorite garbage heap. But what could I do against a grown man? He sneered when he saw me. I ran to try to find a policeman again, but when I am returning, the White Rat is gone." Nura paused, and her lip trembled. "I came to the Needle, even though I had nothing to deliver, because I was thinking maybe

Colonel Battersea could help me. I saw you then," she said at length. "I watched you reach the circle and hide in the bushes. I waited, wondering who you were. I had decided to come to you, but then the Hashashin stepped into the circle."

"I thought we were goners for sure." William nodded.

Nura smiled for the first time. She pursed her lips and repeated the shrill warble.

"That was you?" William said. "It sounded like some kind of strange bird."

"It is a signal used by the Hashashin," Nura replied.

The cousins blinked in surprise, regarding the girl with a mixture of respect and reservation.

"When you found us, what made you so sure we weren't Hashashin, too?" asked Maxine.

"The enemy takes many forms," said Nura, "but I did not think two children hiding in a bush were cause for fear."

"Oh no?" snapped Maxine. "Well, you were plenty afraid of something. What's so precious about this package of yours, anyhow?"

Nura raised an eyebrow. "You told me Colonel Battersea sent you to collect it," she said cautiously, "and yet you don't know what it contains?"

Her hand went to a blue stone that she wore at her throat—a flat glass disk with concentric blue circles that looked like a staring eye—and she shook her head and would speak no further.

"Maybe we should get out of the city," Maxine whispered to William. "If we hurry, we might catch the last train."

Behind her Nura's mouth tightened in a thin, obstinate line. "We cannot leave without the package," she said.

William looked back and forth between the two girls, wondering which of them to listen to. "I wish Grandpa were here," he said. "He'd know what to do."

Maxine grimaced. "Let's just hope he's all right."

"Something has happened to Colonel Battersea?" asked Nura with alarm.

"A couple of men grabbed him at the train station," William admitted. "That was the last we saw of him."

Nura uttered an oath in Turkish and paced the sidewalk. "We cannot leave the city," she said at last.

"Well, we certainly can't stay here," replied Maxine. "We shouldn't even be in the city in the first place. Grandpa only brought us along because he had to. He never meant for us to be wandering around out here all on our own. It's better if we go back and wait for him at Battersea Manor."

Nura shook her head. "Your grandfather will not return home," she said with chilling certainty. "The enemy has him now; his life hangs by a thread. If you want to see him again, we must recover the parcel. It is the only way."

"I don't get it," said Maxine. "How did Grandpa get involved in all of this anyhow? He's supposed to be retired."

Nura twisted her shawl around her thumb, and for a moment the cousins thought she might explain, but instead she closed her eyes and sighed.

"Go if you will," she said, "but I must stay. Tomorrow

I will return to the harbor to look for the White Rat. It is your grandfather's only hope."

The cousins watched Nura make her bed on a hard park bench, unwrapping her headscarf and covering herself as best she could.

"So what's the plan?" Maxine asked in a low voice. "Are we spending the night here with our new friend?"

William bit his thumbnail and pondered their predicament thoughtfully.

"Do you trust her, Will?" asked Maxine.

"I'm not sure. I don't think she's telling us everything. Where did she learn that secret whistle? And what do you make of that strange necklace she's wearing?"

"It looks sort of like an eyeball, doesn't it?"

William nodded. " '*Seek the Needle, find the Eye,*' " he said.

The recollection of the riddle slowed them both for a moment.

"Is that necklace what we were supposed to find?" asked Maxine with a doubtful frown.

"Who knows?" said William. "The necklace, or maybe the girl. I wonder what she's doing here all by herself. She's a million miles from home."

"I don't know," replied Maxine. "Somehow I don't think Grandpa was expecting the courier to be a twelve-year-old girl."

"She seems to think the package is pretty important, though, doesn't she? She's got her own reasons for wanting it back, I'll bet—something more than just helping us track down Grandpa."

"So why should we do her dirty work for her?" said Maxine. "Let her find it herself. I'll take my chances back at the manor any day over playing hide-and-seek in the city with that creep from the tunnel."

"What if she's right, though, M? What if that package really is our only chance to find Grandpa?" William turned his back for a moment and stared at the small girl on the bench. "Did you ever come to a fork in the road and get the feeling that whatever path you chose was bound to be the wrong one?" he asked. Not waiting for an answer, he shoved his hands deep in his pockets and ambled toward Nura.

Maxine watched him go. She knew her cousin well enough by now to guess that he had already decided to stay. She knew herself well enough to realize that, despite her doubts, she would stick with him, that his choice would be her choice, even though it was all perfectly absurd.

She followed William halfheartedly and joined him in front of the park bench, her hands on her hips.

"What will you say to the thief?" she asked Nura, who was already half-asleep. "If you find your White Rat again somehow, what will you say? *May I please have my package back?* How do you know he hasn't already gotten rid of it? Sold it or something?"

Nura sat up abruptly. "Has he sold it?" she said, her voice

shrill as if she were confronting the thief already. "I do not think so. But if he no longer possesses the parcel, he will know who does, and he will tell me, and I will follow, and I *must* follow, and I will never stop until it comes to me again, and from me to Colonel Battersea." Her voice had risen almost to a hysteria, and her eyes were glassy and wide.

"Easy, kiddo," said William, sitting down and putting his arm around her shoulders. "Don't give yourself a nosebleed. You talked us into it, all right? We'll help you get your package back."

CHAPTER 14

The cousins and their new companion woke the next morning with sore necks and foggy heads and no clear memory of where they were. They opened their eyes and sat bolt upright in alarm. A shabby drifter carrying a bindle on the end of an old axe handle was shuffling around the pavilion, eyeing them with interest in the pale light of dawn.

"Bite to eat in there, by any chance?" he asked, pointing at Nura's haversack. "Haven't sunk my teeth into a thing in two days. Gospel truth."

Nura shook her head tensely, pulling the sack tight under her arm, and the man responded with a philosophical shrug. "It's a bad habit," he said, nibbling off a bit of his fingernail and spitting it over his shoulder. "Sleeping on park benches, I mean. Nothing for youngsters."

The children shifted uncomfortably.

"Ain't you seen the papers? There's cutthroats loose in the city. Two nights ago they murdered a police sergeant down on Maiden Lane. Two days before that, it was a carpet merchant in Brooklyn. Police don't have a clue."

He looked the three of them over and shook his head, then turned at last and wandered off.

Maxine clutched her hand to her nose and mouth. "He smelled terrible," she said, watching the drifter leave.

"We've slept too long," said Nura. "We should have been at the harbor already. The White Rat may have come and gone without our knowing, and the package with him."

Above them, the skies had filled with clouds, and through the trees they could see a few early visitors to the park glancing upward and fumbling with their umbrellas. Maxine pulled her mother's red hat down tight and held out her palm to catch the opening notes of a May shower, while Nura wrapped her scarf around her head and shouldered her haversack, starting off without looking back.

William glanced at Maxine and shrugged, and the two of them rose from their benches and trotted after.

They hurried downtown under a steady rain that bloomed in perfect circles in the puddles on the street. Nura pulled a few coins from her bag, and they caught the Broadway trolley, which brought them all the way to Battery Park, to the gray harbor and the ships moored there, to the pier where the parcel was stolen.

Across the waves Lady Liberty held her pale green torch aloft and searched the horizon while the children sat and waited and the morning passed into afternoon.

A ferry landed from Ellis Island. A great press of tired, damp souls churned into the city, clutching their every earthly possession, glancing side to side in uncertainty as they pondered what might come next and then moved on.

William and Maxine sat beneath a steady drizzle and watched the passing crowds. They began to believe they had come on a fool's errand, that Nura's thief would never darken this dock again. But just when they had convinced themselves that the entire day had been wasted, a particular individual among the host of weary immigrants caught William's eye.

It was a young man, a gangling, disagreeable-looking sort, wearing a white suit that rode high at the wrists and ankles and set him apart from the drab crowd like a pale scarecrow. He had a vulgar face with a wisp of a mustache, and a prominent Adam's apple, and he moved among the skittish population of the Battery with a predatory air.

William pinched the girls, and their sagging eyelids snapped open. He jerked his head toward the man, and Nura's face went rigid.

"The White Rat," she said.

The thief wandered the waterfront, casing the park, then turned and angled toward a huddle of young women in tattered shawls, sprawling on a bench behind them with a heavy sigh and a sideways glance. He popped a match with his fingernail, lit a cigarette, and pretended to stare off into the distance.

The cluster of women glanced uneasily at the White Rat and edged away, and he tossed his spent match aside and cursed under his breath, surveying the park for less wary prey.

His eye fell on Nura, who had been watching his charade with disgust. He smoothed an eyebrow and gave her a sneer, then rose and sauntered off, leaving a sickly-sweet waft of pomade in his wake.

The cousins sat frozen in indecision, but Nura sprang to her feet and motioned wildly for them to follow.

The white hat bobbed away, and the three children raced after, doing their best to stay out of sight. Hiding in doorways and behind street-corner postboxes, they darted through the constant stream of pedestrians on the sidewalk until the chase led them several blocks from the Battery, where the wet streets turned dank and desolate.

The afternoon was dwindling. The White Rat turned off the waterfront down a lonesome boulevard lined by burned-out buildings and vacant lots overgrown with withered, whispering grass. The factories and warehouses here lacked the rigid perpendicularity of the living part of the city and loomed ponderously over the three children with a gothic malevolence. From a rooftop nearby they heard the cooing of a dove, and the sound was hollow and unearthly to their ears. If there were monsters in the city, this was where they lurked.

The White Rat stopped at a boarded-up warehouse. In the light of a bare bulb, he glanced over both shoulders and descended into a gloomy stairwell.

"Now what?" said William.

"Let's just wait a minute," Maxine replied. "Maybe he'll come back out."

They stood and watched from a distance, listening to the steady patter of the rain. Nura shivered and fingered the blue pendant that dangled at her neck.

"What is that thing, anyways?" asked William.

"Oh," said Nura, dropping her hand self-consciously. "It is nothing. It is a *nazar boncugu*—a charm against the Evil Eye."

William bent forward and examined it skeptically.

"It preserves the wearer from harm or evil," she explained, "especially from a covetous glance. In my country we say that when someone looks with envy on something precious to you, they bring upon it the curse of the Evil Eye, and it will soon be stolen or lost or grow sick and die. So we keep the *nazar* as protection."

"No kidding," said William. "Were you wearing it when you lost the package?"

Nura nodded solemnly.

"Well then, you might want to take it to a repair shop," he said with a grin.

Nura scowled at him, then couldn't help smiling, too. "Perhaps I do need a new one," she said. She held the charm to her ear and rattled it like a broken watch.

The rain fell yet. Somewhere far off in the city a car

horn honked, but a ghostly canopy of fog dampened every sound.

"Looks like the White Rat is staying put," said Maxine finally.

"Come on, let's go take a closer look," William replied. "We didn't walk all this way for nothing."

CHAPTER 15

Nura and the cousins crossed the street and peered down into the dark stairwell. At the bottom of the steps they could make out a small window on an unmarked steel door that seemed oddly substantial and secure for an abandoned building.

"Go take a peek in that window while I see if there's another way into this place," said William.

Maxine and Nura glanced around warily and descended the stairs, tiptoeing past the steel door as if it were a sleeping crocodile. They tried to look in the window but found it plastered over with old newspapers.

"I can't see a thing," said Maxine, turning to leave. "Let's go and find Will."

No sooner had she uttered the words than she heard a faint scrape behind her. In a blink, the White Rat pounced from beneath the stairs and caught the girls by their collars.

They screamed and tried to wrench free, but he dragged them toward the door.

"Look what we got here," he snarled. "Two of the three blind mice. Let's see if we can't find ourselves a carving knife."

"Let us go!" demanded Nura.

"Please," Maxine begged. "You'll never see us again, I promise."

The White Rat laughed and kicked the steel door twice with a ringing echo.

A hefty doorman in a striped suit opened the door, and the White Rat shoved the girls inside, where they fell in a heap.

Rough hands pulled them to their feet and herded them across the floor. A man with liverish lips and a double chin bound their wrists behind them with baling wire and trussed them up back-to-back against a steel column in the middle of a lofted enclosure.

Maxine cast her eyes about their bleak confinement, fighting off tears. The space where they were tied was dank and sparse. A line of cots stood in the far corner, and a handful of ladder-back chairs were arranged around a dingy green carpet. Long rows of wooden barrels flanked a garage door at the far end of the room, and a blue haze of cigar smoke hung heavy in the air.

A dozen or so men occupied the warehouse, a jury of dark suits and stubbled faces that regarded their guests with calculated apathy. Some stood in the shadows, some lounged around card tables or sat atop barrels, but every eye was on the two girls.

Then the ranks parted to make way for a new face, a thick-necked man wearing a holstered pistol over his starched shirt. His broad shoulders blotted out the weak light behind him.

"What's all this?" he asked.

"Brats just showed up on our doorstep," said the White Rat with a shrug. "Guess maybe they're selling cookies for the Girl Scouts."

"No kidding. Just showed up, huh?" said the man. He gave them a long once-over and scratched his head in irritation. "You two lost or something?" he asked.

The girls were silent.

"I *axed* you a question," he growled. "What are you doing in my warehouse?"

Maxine stammered, trying to buy time for her panicked brain to invent a plausible answer, but Nura spoke up first.

"You have something that belongs to us," she said, her voice low and defiant. "A leather satchel."

Maxine cringed, but the man raised an amused eyebrow. "You don't know who you're talking to, do you, kid?" he said. He bent his neck until it cracked, and then he tapped his chest. "Name's Binny. Binny Benedetti. Around here I'm the top dog, the final authority, the big stick, and the last word. And these are my boys. Papers call us . . . well, they call us a lotta things, but around town it's just the Benedetti outfit."

He stroked his chin. "We don't get many visitors," he said. "'Specially not ones who come barging in with accusations about stolen satchels."

"It was him," snapped Nura, inducing a moan from Maxine. "The White Rat. He stole it from me at the harbor."

"The White Rat," said Binny. A wide grin spread on his cash-drawer underbite. "That's a good one, eh, fellas? That's ST, kid. He's got a weakness for grabbing handbags and rolling drunks, so we call 'im Small Time—ST for short. But maybe he's ready for a new moniker."

He eyed the thief reproachfully. "You know anything about a stolen bag, ST?"

The White Rat stared at the two girls and sucked his gums behind lips that seemed not quite substantial enough to cover his teeth.

"Well, don't just stand there," barked Binny. "Go get 'em their toy."

ST stalked off toward a side room and disappeared through a shabby black door. A moment later he returned, carrying a worn leather satchel. He dangled it in front of Nura sadistically, then tossed it to Binny.

The gangster opened the satchel and produced a battered cigar box tied with a string. He held the box close to his ear and gave the contents a shake. "What do you know 'bout this thing?" he asked, untying the string and opening the lid slightly to peer inside. "It's shiny, sure enough, but it ain't gold."

"It's mine!" Nura growled.

"Not anymore, kid," said Binny, taking a step closer. "I have a feeling you might be able to tell me all about it, though." He tapped her on the forehead. "Or am I wrong?"

Nura seethed, staring daggers at the gangster.

"You're as mad as a meat axe, aren't you?" he said to her, chuckling. "I like that. Passion. Fire. That's something I understand. But you shouldn't oughta get so worked up about it. This's all just for grins an' giggles, see? You gotta think of it like a game.

"The thing is, in this game, I hold all the cards an' you got just one—that being whatever you can tell me about the contents of this bag. Play your card wisely an' you might save your necks. You don't spill your guts, though, then maybe I spill 'em for you. Know what I mean?"

The girls made no response.

"I'd do it slow," he said, his eyes glittering convincingly enough, "and then I'd throw you in some old shack and put a match to it. Let 'er burn till the only thing left of the pair of you is a puddle of grease."

He paused for effect, and the room was silent.

"So you two canaries got one chance to save your tail feathers, and that's for you to start singing."

ST smirked at a slick-haired thug beside him and whispered something in his ear.

"Something funny, ST?" asked Binny. "Maybe you'd like to share it with the whole group."

"Naw, just seems like maybe we're wasting time, Binny. Why not let me an' Clem here take care of these kids for you? This trinket, too, for that matter?"

Binny's eyes narrowed, and he glared at ST suspiciously. "Do me a favor," he said. "Next time some bright idea crosses your conk, keep it to yourself."

ST spit on the floor, and Binny's attention returned to

Nura. "Now, where were we?" he asked, scratching his head. "Oh yeah." He snapped his fingers and nodded at the satchel.

"It is of no value to you or anyone else in this place," said Nura. For a moment she seemed more desperate than defiant. "It is a worthless, evil thing."

There was a knock at the front door of the warehouse, but Binny's eyes were fixed on Nura.

"Not worthless, kid," he said at last. "Not worthless to you, not worthless to ST, apparently. And maybe not worthless to a couple other people around this town."

The doorman ducked away to answer the door and disappeared briefly outside the warehouse. When he returned, he held his hands wide and shrugged.

"It's that crazy ol' gink, the Pigeon," he said.

Binny chewed his lip, still staring at the girls. "Looks like you got yourselves a few minutes to think things over," he said. "I have some business to conduct. We'll finish our little conversation later."

A rangy, stooped individual stamped into the warehouse, dripping wet. He wore a high-collared oilskin coat spangled with silver clasps, and his lank hair was swept back from his balding forehead and tucked behind his ears. A prominent, arched nose protruded from under a pair of rain-spattered motorcycle goggles.

He cocked his head in the girls' direction, and the goggles caught the light like burnished coins.

"Silver bells and cockle shells," he said with a cackle, "and pretty maids all in a row. You working over little girls now, Binny-B?"

"Just business," said Binny with annoyance. "Things that gotta be taken care of." He waved his hand dismissively. "What do you got for me?"

"Right and tight, business it is, then," said the Pigeon, unfastening the clasps on the front of his shining-wet coat and removing a fat envelope from an inside pocket. "Special delivery from Tommy Switches and the Saint. They want to know if you can have ten barrels down at the Indigo Room tonight."

He handed the envelope over and made a notation in a small black book.

Binny counted a thick stack of bills and nodded. "Yeah, we can do that," he said. "Do me a favor and stick around till we get it loaded. I want you to tell Tommy everything was all square when you saw it leave our place."

"You're the boss, Boss," replied the Pigeon, saluting with a knuckle.

Binny returned the cigar box to the satchel and handed it back to ST. "Put this in the john, and then take a walk up the street an' grab the truck," he said.

ST nodded and disappeared, and Binny turned to his doorman. "Have the Lip get on the blower with our friends down at Sixes," he said. "I don't want no excitement this time. If Jimmy Doherty's boys get wind of this, we just keep on driving—got it?

"The rest of you bring the barrels down to the garage door. Not the coffin varnish—the good stuff."

Binny glared at Maxine and Nura, conveying a telepathic threat, then turned to concern himself with the details of the delivery.

For the first time since their arrival, the two girls found themselves alone in the middle of the warehouse. Seizing the opportunity, they began working desperately to free themselves from their bonds. They writhed and strained, but the baling wire only bit deeper into their wrists, and finally they slumped against the steel column in resignation.

Maxine closed her eyes and sighed. "Nura," she said, "I'm sorry about how I treated you when we met. I'm afraid I wasn't very kind. I wish we could start over." She twisted her head, trying to see Nura's face behind her. "I just—I just really wanted to do something right. I had a crazy idea that maybe I could bring Grandpa the package myself. Make him proud. I guess I wanted him to think . . ."

"To think what?"

"I don't know, to think that I was smart. Special. *Useful.*"

"I'm sure you are all those things," said Nura. "You are here with me now when you might have left, and that makes you very useful to me."

Maxine flushed gratefully, but her smile died on her lips.

"Yeah, well, that's more than I can say for Will," she muttered. "I can't believe he just left us stranded here."

There was a pregnant pause.

"Maybe not," said Nura suddenly.

Maxine craned her neck and lifted her eyes to a catwalk below the warehouse ceiling. There in a dark corner just beneath the rafters, she made out a small door along the outer wall. It was opening slowly, and William's head appeared, looking left, then right, checking the room cautiously.

Maxine caught her breath, and her eyes darted anxiously to Binny and his men at the far side of the warehouse.

William edged to the railing and surveyed the floor below. Spotting the girls, he put his finger to his lips and crept toward a rickety staircase at the end of the loft. The wooden stairs groaned beneath him, and the girls flinched, certain that he would be heard, but the gangsters continued their work without pause.

William disappeared from view, and then a minute later they could feel damp fingers fumbling with the wire on their wrists.

"How'd you get in here?" asked Maxine in a low voice.

"I climbed a fire escape out back. Why'd you have to go and get yourselves caught?"

"Shhh! Just get us out of this place, will you?"

"All right, all right. These guys are real trouble, huh? I'm pretty sure those aren't squirt pistols they're wearing under their—"

He stopped midsentence, and all three raised their heads. At that moment, at the end of the warehouse, the garage door opened to the night with a metallic screech. A pair of headlamps blazed outside, igniting a thousand falling raindrops. An engine revved ominously.

Binny stood with his hands on his hips, bathed in the brilliance of the two beams. A dark green delivery truck rolled through the garage door and stopped just inside the warehouse. ST climbed down from the driver's seat.

"What took you so long?" asked Binny. "You oughta been back a while ago."

"We made a little detour," said ST. He walked back and pounded on the side of the truck. "I decided to pick up a few friends."

The cargo door opened with a rattle, and a dozen men descended from the back of the truck with Tommy guns and sawed-down twelve-gauges, spreading out on either side of ST.

"Hey, those are Jimmy Doherty's boys!" snarled the doorman, reaching for his pistol.

Binny nodded. "Looks like I got a rotten apple in the bunch," he said grimly. "Caesar had Brutus, and I got the White Rat."

"You're old and fat, Binny," called ST. "A flat tire. Somebody shoulda put you out to pasture a long time ago."

But Binny was the picture of tranquility. His heavy lids were half closed, as if he were on the verge of sleep. "That day may be coming," he replied with a nod. "I don't figure you'll be around to see it, though."

"Get in the truck, Binny," said ST. "We're going for a little ride."

The gangster raised his head abruptly, and he was changed—his brass and swagger and broad New York diction were cast off, exposing a creature of cunning and violence.

"Do I look like a chump to you?" Binny said, his eyes igniting like an acetylene torch. "Do I look like a rube? Do you think I've survived all these years, outlasted all the two-bit upstarts in this town, only to be chased outta my own house with a rolled-up newspaper by a punk like you?"

He drew his revolver and leveled it at the traitor. "You're full of big ideas, kid, but it'll be a while before a piddling whelp can knock me off the hill. If you think you're ready, though, why then, go ahead and give it a shot."

A whisper of uncertainty crossed the White Rat's face, but he mustered a sneer, and the shadow passed. He wiped his nose on his sleeve and raised his own pistol in answer.

Twenty paces separated the two men, nothing more. Neither of them looked for cover. They eyed each other steadily across the warehouse floor, their faces lit with a murderous fire.

Nura and Maxine had been watching the drama unfold from a distance, holding their breath along with everyone else in the warehouse, but suddenly they felt the baling wire drop from their numb wrists.

"Come on!" whispered William, tugging desperately at their sleeves. "Nobody's watching the front door. Now's our chance!"

CHAPTER 16

The cousins turned and started for the door, but, looking back, they saw that Nura was not with them.

"Nura!" called Maxine in a low, urgent voice. "The exit's this way!"

"Yes, but the package is not," said Nura. She shook her head and dashed off in the other direction.

William and Maxine hesitated for just an instant, then shrugged at each other and turned to follow.

The peeling black door where ST had disappeared earlier with the leather satchel was situated beneath the catwalk, at the end of a long row of canvas-draped crates. Nura crouched, hugging the wall, and William and Maxine followed close behind, keeping a wary eye on the situation brewing around the truck.

They reached their goal and tried the handle, but the black door was stuck. Nura put her shoulder into it—gently, so as not to make a sound—and the three children tumbled inside a dingy bathroom onto a grimy tile floor. A handful of white moths made drunken circles around a lightbulb on the ceiling above, and the stall door in front of them hung limply on buckled hinges. A filthy ashtray, overflowing with cigar butts, sat balanced on the corner of the sink.

Nura leapt to her feet and began rummaging about the room. She went through a dented waste bin and checked beneath the sink, but the leather bag was nowhere to be found. Her face lit up, though, as she glanced in the mirror above the dripping faucet. There in the streaked glass she saw the satchel hanging from a coat hook on the door behind them.

Whirling around, she sprang to the bag, opening it in a heartbeat and straining to make out the contents in the dim light.

"Is it in there?" asked Maxine, crowding close behind her.

Nura removed the old cigar box and breathed a great sigh of relief. "Yes," she said. "It is safe."

She slung the empty bag over her shoulder and was about to place the cigar box back inside, but Maxine stopped her.

"Wait a minute," she said, snatching the satchel. "Maybe Binny and ST don't have to know we took the package." She grabbed the ashtray from the corner of the sink and dumped the contents inside the leather bag, and then, for good measure, she dumped the ashtray in as well.

"At least this way they won't figure out anything is missing from the bag until they open it up," she said. "It might give us a head start." She returned the satchel to its hook, and Nura nodded approvingly.

William pressed his ear against the black door and grasped the handle, but at that instant a ringing concussion on the other side made him recoil as if the knob were red-hot. The trio froze for a moment, then backed away from the door. Out in the warehouse they heard a string of shots—ten, maybe twelve—all in the time it takes to blow out a match.

A great commotion followed. Curses and running feet and the caustic smell of spent shells. The truck engine coughed to life.

"We can't go out there," William whispered in alarm.

"There must be some other way," said Maxine. She glanced around the room, then down at the floor. At her feet a handful of shadows wove dizzy circles in a sallow puddle of light. She glanced up suspiciously at the moths that flitted around the bare bulb.

"How do you figure *they* got in here?" she asked.

Without waiting for an answer, she pushed open the crippled stall door. Just above the water tank behind the toilet was a small, dusty window, open a crack. Outside, the lights of the city winked in the distance.

Another volley of angry shouts erupted in the warehouse, and Nura hugged the cigar box close to her chest. "They know we are missing," she said.

Maxine motioned toward the open window. William

nodded, pushing Nura through the stall door and boosting her unceremoniously onto the tank above the toilet.

"Time to go," he said.

An eight-foot drop later, William and the girls stood in a shining-wet alley behind the warehouse. Nura wiped the grit from a bloodied knee, and the three of them bolted off into the night.

The skies were clearing; the Hare Moon glinted through the breaks in the skidding clouds. In the distance, the sun-burst of the unfinished Chrysler Building rose high above Midtown like an eternal flame, a beacon of true north. They galloped on, away from the deserted backstreets toward the living city, with only the sound of their own pounding foot-steps for company.

Two blocks up a familiar green delivery truck passed through the intersection, driving slowly. The children ducked behind a sidewalk newsstand as it vanished from sight; then they sprinted off once more, past shuttered jew-elry shops and empty delicatessens and a darkened church that regarded their coming and going with monastic indif-ference.

Maxine halted finally, beside the steps of a corner barbershop. "I have to stop," she gasped. "Just for a minute."

They leaned heavily on their knees and gulped for air. Somewhere far behind them a dog barked belligerently, touching off a chorus of yaps and howls that swelled above the city.

Nura slumped down on the wet steps and clutched the parcel to her chest.

"We did it, didn't we, Nura?" whispered Maxine, covering her mouth in a kind of elated disbelief. "We got the package! We got the package, and we're still in one piece!"

Nura laid her palms on the cigar box and stared at it for a long while.

"So when do we get to see what's in there?" asked William. He elbowed Nura in the ribs, but she only blinked vacantly, and her hands never moved.

"Come on, Nura," begged Maxine. "I think I'll positively have kittens if you don't open it!"

Nura gave her a weak smile, and then, slowly and deliberately, she untied the string around the package.

They peered at it in the sickly light of the corner streetlamp.

"You didn't travel six thousand miles just to deliver a box of cigars, I hope," said William.

Nura ignored him and lifted the lid with trembling fingers, and the cousins gazed at last upon the strange object for which they had risked their lives. Until this moment they had known it only by its influence and aura—the violent greed it had stirred in Binny and ST, the longing and dread it held for Nura, the urgency it had spurred in Grandpa. Now that it was unveiled before their own eyes, they found themselves strangely unsettled in its presence.

A shining object glinted inside the box, nestled atop a folded length of black silk. Nura tugged at the end of the wide silk ribbon, piling several feet of it in her lap, then lifted the flashing silver article to which the black ribbon was attached, dangling it in front of them.

It was a mirror, slightly larger than a tea saucer and dusky, its lustrous surface polished to a flawless reflection. The metal disk had been cast in one piece, without frame or handle, and an image of the crescent moon was engraved upon it, embracing the silvered face within its pointed horns. Nura turned the disk over to reveal a swirling confusion of Arabic calligraphy that licked flamelike across the opposite side, interrupted by five staring eyes carved amid the chaos. A series of irregular slits were fashioned along the outer edge, and through one of these the long black sash was tied.

It was an extraordinary object—a worthy addition to Grandpa's basement collection—but looking at her dark reflection in its polished surface, Maxine shrank back inexplicably. The thing was not pleasant to her sight.

"What is it?" William asked.

"The Eye of Midnight," replied Nura. "The Key to Paradise."

"We saw a strange telegram back at Battersea Manor that mentioned an Eye," whispered Maxine. "'*Seek the Needle, find the Eye,*' that's what it said. We thought maybe it meant your necklace."

"No," said Nura. "This is the Eye of which the telegram spoke."

"Is it magic?" asked William. "Grandpa told us a story about a magic mirror that belonged to an old jinni."

"Magic?" said Nura. "Who knows for certain? But it is not belonging to any jinni. It is his—the Old Man of the Mountain. He wears the mirror next to his heart, bound to his bosom with the black silk sash. In its darkened glass, the Hashashin believe the Old Man sees all things past, present, and future. It is the holiest of objects to him and to his servants—the Key to the Garden of Paradise and the symbol of his power over the *fida'i*."

"The who?" asked William.

"The *fida'i*—the Old Man's destroying angels. They are the faithful, the living daggers of the desert fortress of Al-amut. Within the ranks of the Hashashin, it is the *fida'i* who carry out the master's bloody bidding. For him, willingly and unquestioningly, they will give their lives, and with their curving daggers they will kill."

Nura paused and polished the mirror with her sleeve.

"Put it back," said Maxine with a shudder.

"What does Grandpa want with it, I wonder?" asked William, watching as Nura swaddled it with the black silk sash. "And why did the Old Man ever give it away?"

"He is not giving it to anyone," she answered. "It was stolen from him."

"Stolen? By who? And how did you end up with it?"

Nura looked at the cousins with a level stare. She replaced the black bundle in the cigar box, tied it shut carefully, and would say no more.

CHAPTER 17

William rose from the barbershop steps and wandered away from the girls into the empty street.

"So now what, Nura?" he asked, turning back toward the stoop. "I thought you said the mirror would lead us to Grandpa."

"No," she replied, lowering her eyes. "I only said we had no hope of saving him without it."

Maxine stiffened. "You can take us to him, though, can't you?" she asked anxiously. "You can find him?"

Nura laid a finger behind a wet pebble and nudged it off the step. "I do not know where he is," she said.

"Then it was all for nothing!" Maxine cried. "We risked our lives to get the package back, and all we have to show for it is wet clothes and skinned knees. We're no closer to getting out of this fix than we were before."

"I had hoped that when we found the Eye of Midnight we would find Colonel Battersea as well," Nura said.

"Well, that's just fine," said Maxine hollowly. "Only all we turned up was a bunch of gangsters."

William kicked at a scrap of rusty can in the gutter. "Doesn't that seem a little strange?" he said. "What would Binny and his gang want with a weird old mirror?"

"I cannot say," answered Nura. "It is an ancient relic, belonging to a different world. It has nothing to do with them."

"Then why were you bringing the mirror to Grandpa?" asked Maxine. "It has nothing to do with him either, does it?"

"My mother and father sent me to deliver the Eye of Midnight to Colonel Battersea," replied Nura. "They told me he would know how to help."

"No offense," said William, lifting an eyebrow, "but why didn't they just bring it to him themselves? Seems like maybe they shouldn't have sent you off all on your own."

Nura's face fell. She turned away and tried to master herself, but her lip quivered, and she covered her eyes with her hand. Tears rolled down her cheeks like drops of hot wax.

William winced and scratched the back of his neck, wondering what he had said. "Forget about it, Nura," he muttered. "I'm sorry I mentioned it." He shook her shoulder gently. "Things aren't so bad. We got the mirror back, didn't we? All we have to do now is track down Grandpa." He looked her in the eye and forced a smile. "We'll find him soon. We'll find him and be back at Battersea Manor safe and sound before you know it," he said, raising two fingers. "Scout's honor."

It was a reckless promise, of course. Anyone inclined to superstition would be quick to point out that even uttering such a notion aloud was a foolishness, that audacity of this stripe could only ever have ended in catastrophe. In truth, however, there was no indication that William's impertinence played any part in what happened next. Certainly no fateful sign materialized. No black cat or cackling raven appeared. The moon did not darken. In fact, the only omen of impending calamity came in the form of a faint and curious noise.

Nura heard it first. A fading echo on the wet streets, a muffled, indistinguishable sound. She lifted her head and dried her eyes.

"What is it?" asked Maxine.

Nura shook her head and listened, and they all heard it then: a faint growl that rose and fell unpredictably on the breeze. By some trick of the empty, echoing streets, it was difficult to tell where the sound was coming from. Their eyes flitted about the crevices of the city, searching the dim alleys and doorways and balconies that surrounded them.

They thought of diving for cover, but it was too late. All at once the vague growl swelled to a deep rumble. Out of the clotted darkness roared a red motorcycle, and bent low over the handlebars sat a goggled rider in a flapping black coat.

The cycle sped past in a swirling eddy of spray, and William and the girls prayed for the red taillamp to continue on and disappear in the distance, but instead it slowed, and the machine swung in a wide arc, returning to the stoop.

"Salutations, regards, et cetera et cetera," said the rider with a morose nod, pushing his goggles up onto his forehead.

It was the Pigeon.

"Swallowed your tongues, eh?" he said, watching them closely. "Well, let's hope your legs still work. The Benedetti gang is out here somewhere looking for you, you know."

"Wh-what happened to them?" asked William. "To Binny and ST?"

"I didn't wait to find out, to be honest. When the bullets start to fly, I make it a habit not to stick around."

"But you—you work for Binny, don't you?"

"I work for all the gangs in town, kid. I stay alive 'cause I don't get involved. I don't play favorites, and I don't flap my gums. Never took a bribe and never missed a drop. I do know what's what, though, and I know the three of you need to get yourselves out of town. You don't belong here."

"We can't leave," said Maxine. "We've got to find our granddad. Somebody grabbed him at the train station."

The Pigeon tapped one of the gauges between his handlebars. "You mean the old colonel," he said, and he nodded slyly. "I might know something about that."

Nura and the cousins stared at him in disbelief.

The Pigeon made a croaking laugh. "Hickory Dickory, plots and trickery!"

"But how?" said Maxine. "How could you—"

"Like I said, Freckles, I do business with all the gangs in town. Nothing happens that I don't hear about."

Maxine rose from the steps. "Can you take us to him?" she asked.

But the Pigeon stamped his boots and looked away.

"Listen, kid, this is bigger than all of us," he said. "There's a storm coming. A black cloud stretching out in every direction. So let me give you three a piece of advice. Do yourselves a favor and get out of the city. Nothing here for you but broken bones and tombstones."

"Please, we have to find him. Can't you at least tell us where he is?" Maxine pleaded.

The Pigeon muttered an oath under his breath.

"Something evil's sleeping underneath these streets," he said at last, kneading an earlobe restlessly between his thumb and forefinger. "Waiting to devour, and burn, and destroy. It won't stop until it's picking the whole world out of its teeth. If you're hoping to find Granddad, well, then you'll have to enter its lair."

He hacked and spit on the pavement, as if the words had left a foul taste on his lips.

"There's an old graveyard not far from here—the Knickerbocker Plainsong Cemetery. Inside the dike, look for a passing traveler."

"Inside the dike . . . a passing traveler?"

"That's all I got," said the Pigeon, adjusting his goggles. "You already know more than what's good for you."

And with that, the Pigeon stood in his seat and gunned the starter with his heel. The cycle roared to life, and he vanished into the night.

CHAPTER 18

Maxine looked up from her map and glanced over her shoulder at William and Nura. The street ended abruptly before them at a tall, wrought-iron gate. A creaking signboard above the entrance indicated their arrival at the Knickerbocker Plainsong Cemetery.

"You're as good as a slobbery old bloodhound, M," said William.

"Thanks, I think," Maxine replied uneasily.

A low mist had settled inside the fence—a gauzy veil that clung to every headstone and hollow. Tangled vines groped the arched gateway and the crumbling monuments.

They shuffled through the gate in a skittish cluster, their eyes darting about the brooding shapes of the lonely grave-yard.

"Do you see anything?" whispered Nura.

"Plenty," Maxine replied. "Nothing I like, though."

"Maybe the Pigeon had it wrong," said William. "This hardly seems like the kind of place Grandpa would end up."

Their feet squelched in the sodden earth as they crept between the neglected headstones, and the graves all around seemed to press closer as they went, as if the monuments were not quite rooted to the ground.

William turned and eyed the stones closest to him. "'DeBoer . . . Van Kiehle . . . Janssen . . . ,'" he read. "What kind of names are these?"

"Dutch, I think," said Maxine. "New York City was founded by Dutch settlers."

"That's a good sign, I guess—seeing as we're looking for a dike."

"Dike," said Nura. "What does this word mean?"

"I dunno," said William. "It's some kind of dam, I think. Dutch people are s'posed to be crazy for 'em. I remember a story about a little Dutch boy who plugged a hole in a dike with his finger. I never saw anything like that in a graveyard, though."

Maxine pushed William forward, and they continued on, hunched low like scavengers on a moonlit battlefield. They reached the back fence of the cemetery but found no ditches, pools, or dikes, only a silent boulevard of decrepit crypts that jutted from the hanging fog. Beyond these the hulking shape of a darkened factory loomed distant in the mist.

"End of the line," William said to Maxine, conceding defeat. Nura wandered on, though, roaming the long row of the houses of the dead, reading the names inscribed on each.

She stopped at the largest of the crypts. A carved pair

of weeping figures guarded the door, their hooded faces bent toward the ground.

She called the cousins with a low whistle, and pointed to the name inscribed on the lintel.

"'Van Dyck,'" read Maxine.

"That's it, Nura!" cried William with unconcealed admiration. "*Inside the dike* . . . You found it! This has to be the dike that the Pigeon was talking about!"

"Maybe." Nura shrugged. "Maybe it is nothing."

"What now?" asked Maxine.

"We go inside, I guess," replied William.

Maxine paled. "Into the tomb? But it's sealed shut."

William stepped up to the door and laid his hands against the stone. A carved skull stared him in the face, grinning above a solemn verse:

Take heed, Wanderer,
As thou art, so I once was,
As I am, so shalt thou be.

"There's a cheerful thought," he muttered.

He gave the door a halfhearted push, expecting frozen resistance, but to his surprise, it swung open easily.

Maxine and Nura clutched the back of his jacket, peering over his shoulder.

"What do you see?" asked Nura.

"I can't make out a thing. It's pitch-dark in there."

The inside of the crypt was indeed as black as a cannon

bore. William fumbled in his pocket for the box of matches he had been carrying ever since they left the manor. He fished it out and labored to strike a light in the damp air, but soon the flame popped and flared. Three pulses fluttered weakly as the children clutched their hands to their mouths and shuffled one by one through the doorway.

The air inside the tomb was musty and stale. A layer of grit dusted the floor, crunching underfoot as they went, and William's flame revealed two rows of stone coffins separated by a narrow aisle.

"You don't think Grandpa is . . . ," said William, laying his hand on one of the rectangular boxes, "I mean, he can't be—"

"Shush," said Maxine. "There's something carved on the lids."

William held the flame close to the top of the nearest sarcophagus, and then to its matching twin across the aisle.

What is the word?
The tongue's keen arrow.

"It's some sort of riddle," said Maxine, studying the lids. "Questions on one side, answers on the other."

The match burned low, singeing William's finger, and he dropped it with a yowl. The girls heard scrabbling in the dark, and then a sharp scratch followed by another yellow flame. They continued down the aisle slowly, reading the lines aloud.

"What is the tongue?
The traitor of the mind,
The blight of the air.

"What is the air?
The sustainer of life.

"What is life?
The joy of the blessed,
The burden of the wretched,
The journey of man."

They reached the back of the crypt and leaned over the final pair of coffins.

What is man?

The flame sputtered and went out.

"'What is man?'" said Nura, prodding William in the back.

"Hold on," he said. "I have to find another match."

He struck the light, sheltering it with his hand as it writhed and twisted, and the three of them bent their heads close over the stone slab.

The slave of death,
A wanderer upon the earth,
A traveler passing.

Nura gasped in surprise, and the weak flame flickered, then went out. The crypt was pitched into utter blackness.

"I hate it in here," muttered Maxine, a mounting terror creeping up her back like a spider under her clothes. She clawed at the buttons on her jacket, which all at once seemed suffocating. "Light another match, Will!"

"That was the last one," he replied shakily.

"The door shut behind us!" Maxine cried, realizing all at once how foolish they had been. She fumbled her way back toward the entrance.

"We're trapped!" she said. "I can't find a handle!"

A voice spoke up in the dark. It belonged to Nura, but the sound of it was cold and strange.

"The way out lies below us," she said. "Beneath the tomb of the passing traveler, just as the Pigeon told us."

"What? You mean we have to open up this box?" asked William.

"Of course not!" Maxine burst out. "That's ridiculous!"

But Nura and William had already found the edge of the lid, and in the darkness Maxine could hear them straining to shift it.

"Well, don't just stand there, M," said William. "Give us a hand."

They all leaned hard against the weight of the lid, and there was a dull grinding sound, a rumble as deep as the planets turning on their axes. The stone slab slid back, and an orange light erupted from the box. Eerie shadows danced hugely on the ceiling of the crypt, and their three faces were cast with a lurid glare as they peered into the tomb. A narrow shaft sank into the ground, empty except for a wooden ladder and a hissing torch lit with a bright flame that fluttered and swayed in the depths below.

They stared down into the pit, their expressions as somber as the figures carved on the outside of the crypt.

William cleared his throat nervously. "Who's first?" he asked.

CHAPTER 19

At the bottom of the hole they found themselves in the mouth of a tunnel of raw earth. Peering down the passageway, they could see no farther than the next burning torch, but Nura prodded the cousins, and they all ventured in single file, holding on to one another like elephants marching a darkened trail.

Their fingertips brushed against walls of rock and clay as they stumbled over loose stones at their feet, past an endless succession of hissing torches, until it felt as if the tunnel were digesting them, pulling them down to the earth's very roots.

"We're lost for sure," said Maxine.

"But the path has never turned or forked," Nura replied.

"Well, we're not under the graveyard anymore, I can tell you that much," Maxine insisted.

William squinted down the murky tunnel. "How much

farther does it go on?" he muttered. But even as he spoke the words the passage widened, ending unexpectedly at a smooth section of hewn stone that looked as if it had been exhumed from long burial. In the middle of the exposed wall stood a heavy wooden door, and branded on the front was a blackened seal: a twelve-pointed star formed of curving daggers.

Nura turned the knob delicately, and the door opened with a creak. Placing a finger to her lips, she motioned for Maxine and William to follow.

They were standing in the mouth of a wide hall that stretched away before them like the nave of a dim cathedral. A scarlet carpet paved the aisle, embroidered with gold vines and blue medallions and the likenesses of serpents and apes. The way was lined on either side with carved pillars that spiraled up into the gloom, each one writ black with words of unknown script and hung with brass lamps that glimmered like flickering tongues. The entire narrow aisle winked with a thousand shifting lights, but outside of the long rows of stone columns to their left and right, the walls of the chamber were lost in shadow.

"What *is* this place?" whispered Maxine.

"A lair," answered Nura, padding forward on the carpet. "The hiding place of evil."

"But it's deserted."

"Deserted? Who then tends the torches and the lamps?"

"So where is everybody?" asked William, his voice echoing throughout the hall.

They stopped and turned about, but nothing stirred, and they continued on.

At the far end of the hall, the carpet expired at a flight of three stairs. The children stepped up and passed beneath a covered porch, then halted at a curtain of beaded strands that glittered with colored stones and tiny silver bells.

Nura parted the beads and put her eye to the gap. She hesitated momentarily before gesturing onward.

They stepped through into a room that was smaller than the last. Smaller, but not small; a room without corners; a room of concentric circles. In the middle of this wide rotunda stood a large, round table draped in a coverlet of loosely woven linen, and on its surface sat a claw-footed brazier that burned bright with a purple flame. All along the room's outer edge was a ring of squat tables scattered with a hundred silken cushions of blue and orange that encompassed the entire chamber.

"Look at the walls," murmured Maxine, turning slowly.

Nura and William lifted their eyes and beheld a magnificent mural that glinted with gems and hammered gold. Peacocks and leopards wandered among crystal fountains; long tables groaned under platters and bowls piled high with delicacies of every kind; young maidens with pale flowers in their hair reclined beneath ivory pavilions; and high above, crimson pennants waved upon a breeze.

"It looks like some kind of picnic in the park," said William.

"The Garden of Paradise," replied Nura. "The eternal reward promised to the Old Man's followers."

Set into the muraled wall was a succession of five evenly spaced niches lit with living flames, and between them five arched doorways. Above each arch was the crude symbol of a strange beast: a scorpion, a winged serpent, a two-headed sphinx, a leopard, and a one-armed, one-legged man.

"Which doorway do we choose?" asked Maxine.

"I don't know. Which one looks like Grandpa might be behind it?"

But even as William spoke the words, Maxine froze and cupped her fingers behind her ear.

Footsteps fell outside the curtain where they had entered.

"Someone's coming!" she whispered, pointing to the hall without.

They all sprang to the middle of the room and leapt beneath the center table, ducking under the linen coverlet just as a knot of men brushed through the beaded curtain. They were clad like desert raiders, in long black cloaks with scarlet sashes double-bound across their chests and staring eyes that burned behind their tightly wound headscarves.

"The *fida'i*," whispered Nura in terror as she peered through the gauzy veil of the tablecloth. "The Old Man's living daggers."

Among this tight cluster was another pair of figures. Their dress was western, and they seemed entirely out of place among the cloaked *fida'i*.

Nura, William, and Maxine stared through the sheer fabric at the faces of the two men at the center of the huddle.

"What are *they* doing here?" whispered William.

It was Binny and the White Rat. Both looked somewhat worse for wear. Binny's head was held high, but his right eye was swollen shut, and his collar was wet with blood. ST walked in front of him, carrying the leather satchel over his shoulder and taking in his surroundings with a wary eye.

One of the *fida'i* struck a ringing note on a large bronze bell that hung near the curtain, and by and by a solitary figure emerged on the far side of the chamber through the doorway marked with the winged serpent. He wore a long, pale mantle trimmed in crimson and a carved-ivory breast-plate figured with the same twelve-pointed star they'd seen branded on the entrance of the lair. A jeweled dagger hung at his waist, and his hooded eyes brought into the room a palpable dissatisfaction.

The *fida'i* bent low and laid three fingers across their foreheads.

"It's him! The specter from the Needle!" whispered William beneath the table. "Is that the Old Man of the Mountain?"

Nura shook her head. "He is the Rafiq, second in command. His silver ring signifies his rank among the Hashashin. He rules the *fida'i* in the Old Man's absence."

"Mr. Benedetti," said the Rafiq with a corrupt smile. "What an unexpected honor." He moved close and fingered the wound on Binny's neck. "As I recall, you scoffed at the suggestion of an alliance last time we spoke," he said with a frown. "But perhaps you are wiser now. Why resist the rising tide? All the others of your kind have bent the knee in allegiance. The Old Man of the Mountain will rule this city, and someday every realm, in every corner of the earth. You would do well to take him for a master and not an enemy."

Binny labored to draw a full breath. "The Old Man can shine my shoes if he'd like," he said with a grunt.

The Rafiq motioned minutely to the *fida'i* on Binny's left and right, and they gripped the wounded man's wrists and spread his arms wide. The Rafiq's hand dropped casually to the gangster's waist, and he unfastened his belt buckle, pulling it free, dangling the length of smooth leather limply in his outstretched hand. His face was vacant as he watched it sway, serpentlike, above the floor, as if the movement itself was a fascination.

All at once, he swung it with breathtaking violence, catching the gangster with the buckle just above the eye.

Binny staggered and sank to his hands and knees, blood streaming down his nose and into his mouth.

The Rafiq tugged at the curl of his long goatee and squatted. "The offer still stands. My master would very much appreciate your allegiance."

Binny licked the blood from his lips and spat defiantly.

"As you like," said the Rafiq, tossing a ring of heavy keys to one of the *fida'i*. "Put him away with the colonel. Let them share the same fate."

Beneath the table, the children's pulses skipped a beat at the mention of Colonel Battersea.

The *fida'i* swept out of the round room through the scorpion doorway, taking Binny with them. The chamber was empty now, except for ST and the Rafiq.

"What have you brought me?" asked the Rafiq, crooking a finger toward the leather satchel.

ST's tongue flicked across his teeth. "I did just like you

said. Kept an eye open down at the harbor for the little girl with the checkered scarf. She showed up the other day, and I grabbed the bag."

Nura and the cousins traded startled glances. The theft of the package had not been a chance encounter after all.

"Indeed?" said the Rafiq, and his eyes glittered. *"Aferin!* Give it to me."

"I would've brought it to you sooner, but Binny got his mitts on it. He said if you wanted it so bad, then he wanted to know why." ST presented the bag to the Rafiq with a mock flourish. "You don't got to worry about him no more, though." He grinned. "I took care of everything. Now you got Binny and your shiny mirror both, all wrapped up and hand-delivered."

The Rafiq grasped the satchel, but ST didn't release it. He gripped it tight and held his ground. "You know, I been thinking," he said slowly, "maybe Binny has a point. Seems like you want this thing awful bad. Maybe I shouldn't oughta just hand it over. I ain't been paid yet for my trouble."

Unearthly shadows flickered over the Hashashin's face in the light of the purple flame.

"All in due time," he said, baring his teeth.

ST stood and pondered his position, measuring up the Rafiq. Reluctantly he surrendered the bag.

The Rafiq's fingers trembled as he unfastened the buckles and reached inside the satchel. His eyes narrowed and his countenance fell as he groped within.

"What is the meaning of this?" he asked, withdrawing his hand and grinding a fine powder between his thumb and forefinger. He upended the satchel, and an acrid cascade of cinders and cigar ends spilled onto the floor along with the dirty ashtray.

ST snatched his hat from his head. His face twisted in an imbecilic grin and he staggered backward.

"It—it was those kids!" he stammered. "The girl I took the satchel from. Her and the other one. They showed up at the warehouse today looking for the bag."

The Rafiq studied the back of his thumb coldly, waiting for the young man to continue.

"We had them all tied up," said ST. "There was some excitement down at the warehouse, though. Things got a little hot when we went to put Binny in the truck. And when it was all over, the kids was gone. Poof! Just up and disappeared. They must have grabbed your mirror on the way out."

The Rafiq opened his hands slightly to indicate that such news did not interest him. He walked slowly to the center of the room and laid his hands flat upon the table. Behind the thin linen cover, Nura and the cousins cringed as they stared at his heavy boots.

"The Old Man of the Mountain requires the Eye of Midnight," he said, his voice calm and composed as he stared into the purple flame. "It is all he thinks of, all he cares for, day and night. It is his most prized possession. And yet you dare to come to me empty-handed, telling stories of magical, disappearing children."

"I can get it for you," said ST. He twisted the brim of his smudged white hat and held it close to his chest. "I found the girl before, and I can do it again," he said, recovering some semblance of his former confidence. "But I risked my neck for your little trinket once already, and I never seen a dime for my trouble." He set his jaw and did his best to draw himself up to his full height. "So like I said, I think maybe it's time I get paid."

A thick vein throbbed in the Rafiq's temple like a sucking leech. He turned and crossed the room, backing ST toward the wall until his beard almost touched the young thief's brow. His eye twitched once, and for the time being the children's view of ST was obscured by the Hashashin's tall frame.

"Yes," he snarled. "Receive your reward." His hand dropped to the jeweled hilt at his waist. "The wages of a fool."

Through the weave of the linen tablecloth they saw a silver flash as the Rafiq's clenched fist passed across the White Rat's throat. He stepped back, and ST swayed gently on his feet, his expression puzzled and glassy, and now the front of his white suit was streaked with a scarlet stain. He looked down and daubed at it clumsily as if it were a soiled necktie. Then he crumpled in a heap, like a marionette whose strings had all been cut in a single pass.

Maxine clapped her hand to her mouth in horror, stifling a gasp, and William and Nura trembled beside her. The Rafiq crouched and wiped his blade clean on the dingy white suit, then rose and withdrew through the door by which he'd come, to the inner recesses of the lair.

CHAPTER 20

William and the girls scrambled out from beneath the table, averting their eyes from the limp form on the far side of the room.

"We must not stay here," said Nura, adjusting her haversack across her shoulder. "Someone will come to carry away the body."

She glanced at the dark passage where the *fida'i* had taken Binny, then crept inside. A moment later she returned, shaking her head.

"There is a locked door within," she said. "The way is blocked."

She took one of the brass lamps from its niche in the wall and made a slow circuit of the room, peeking into the other arched doorways. Choosing the opening beneath the sphinx, she disappeared from view.

"In here," she said, emerging partially and waving them in.

The cousins obeyed, stumbling after her into a gloomy storeroom stacked with basins and crockery. William steadied himself against a heavy butcher's block and reached for a damp rag slung across a nearby water tap. He pressed it to his forehead and passed it to the girls. Feeling somewhat restored, they turned slowly and glanced about their dim surroundings.

The room was full to bursting with provisions: tall urns and bulging sacks, quarters of smoked meat, long shelves sagging with olives and dates and spices, and countless baskets full of nuts and cheeses and eggs and every other thing.

Nura fell on the food ravenously, pushing bread and raisins into her mouth with both hands. She passed the baskets to William and Maxine, and for a few minutes there were no words, only gulping and chewing with barely a space for breath.

At length William swallowed down the last of a bowl of greasy fritters and licked his fingers.

"Did you hear what he said? About locking Binny up with the colonel?"

"I heard," replied Maxine. "Grandpa is here somewhere."

William nodded. "I wish we could get our hands on those keys."

Maxine thought of the lifeless body sprawled on the floor in the next room. "He'll kill us if he catches us, won't he?" she murmured.

"The Rafiq?" said Nura. "Yes. He is *bir canavar*—an ogre."

"He wants the Eye of Midnight pretty bad, though," said William. "Maybe he'll make a trade—Grandpa for the mirror."

"He doesn't seem much like the bargaining type," Maxine replied.

"At least now we know why the gangsters had the mirror, though," said William. "ST was working for the Rafiq."

"It still doesn't make any sense," Maxine said. "Why did the Rafiq need ST in the first place? Why didn't he just send the *fida'i* to the harbor to steal the mirror themselves?"

"The White Rat was a clumsy, ignorant servant," said Nura in agreement.

"It's almost as if the Rafiq was trying to get his hands on the Eye of Midnight without the *fida'i* knowing about it," said Maxine. "He made sure the room was empty before he mentioned it to ST."

William tugged meditatively at a rope of linked sausages. "Maybe we should leave the Rafiq a note," he said. "Tell him we have the Old Man's precious mirror and that we'll hand it over when he lets Grandpa go free."

Nura lowered her head dejectedly and murmured something under her breath.

"What's wrong?" asked William. "Wasn't that the plan? To use the mirror to ransom Grandpa?"

"The mirror might buy his freedom, yes," said Nura. "Though I doubt the Rafiq would honor any promise that he made. But Colonel Battersea is not the Old Man of the Mountain's only prisoner."

"What do you mean?"

Nura hesitated. "I have not told you everything," she said at last, and her cheeks flushed. "You asked me before why my parents had sent me all alone to find Colonel Battersea—why they didn't come themselves. The truth is, they could not. It was impossible."

Her face was hard, and she looked steadily at the cousins. "My parents both lie captive in the desert fortress of Alamut."

"They're prisoners of the Old Man, too?" asked William in surprise. "How? Why?"

"The Hashashin fell on us in the night," said Nura slowly, and the cousins could see in her eyes that she was there now, reliving the terrible moment in her mind. "My parents sacrificed themselves so that I could escape. They had warned me that the Old Man might find us one day, and I knew what I was to do. I saddled our horse and fled for the coast with the Eye of Midnight, not certain if my parents were alive or dead. Only when I reached the household of Yusuf in Alexandretta did I learn that they had been carried away to Alamut."

"Yusuf?" broke in William. "The same Yusuf who sent Grandpa the telegram?"

Nura nodded. "Yusuf is a man my father knew from long ago and trusted. A man he said was a friend of Colonel Battersea's who would be of help if trouble ever found us."

"But why were your parents in trouble in the first place?" asked Maxine. "What did they do to make an enemy of the Old Man of the Mountain?"

"They possessed the Eye of Midnight," said Nura. "That in itself was enough. And when the Old Man had torn apart our home and discovered that the mirror was nowhere to be found, he took my parents as security for its return. Word came to Yusuf of their fate. They lie now in the Dungeons of Paradise, beneath the desert fortress of Alamut. If we give up the mirror to rescue Colonel Battersea . . ."

She paused and shook her head hopelessly.

"If we give up the mirror to rescue Grandpa," said William, "then your last chance of seeing your parents again goes with it."

Nura nodded.

William found an apple in a barrel at his elbow and polished it thoughtfully on his sleeve.

"Well then," he said, "I guess we'll just have to get our hands on those keys."

"Come on," said William at length, rising and brushing the crumbs from his jacket. "Let's see what else is back here."

They wandered deeper in, foraging among the piles of supplies, until they reached the back of the storeroom and the foot of what they first believed to be a set of staggered shelves.

Upon closer inspection, it turned out to be a rickety

wooden staircase—so heavily burdened with jars and sacks and tins that their first conclusion was entirely understandable. Nudging aside a few casks and boxes, they picked their way to the top and bobbed their heads through a dark, rectangular opening in the ceiling above.

They were looking out across an old attic with rough planked floors, and if the quantity of dust and cobwebs was any indication, the Hashashin rarely ventured here. They clambered up, and Nura raised her lamp to dispel the dark. All at once they perceived that the space was much bigger than they had first thought, opening out into a vast enclosure.

Maxine stooped to grasp a soiled paper label that lay at her feet.

THE DEVOITTE CO.
"ADAMANT"
Celebrated Spar Varnish

"We must be in the old factory we saw from the graveyard," she said.

They were, in point of fact, standing amid the rack and ruin of the Devoitte Paint and Varnish Works—a dense jungle of wooden scaffolding and presses, decaying machinery and rusting pipes. The wheels of progress, grinding ever on, had reduced the factory to a dilapidated hulk.

They prowled the creaking floors beneath a skeletal tracery of beams and swagged ropes. Stepping around the end of a long row of battered copper tanks, William happened to glance down at the floor and saw that there, beneath his feet, the rough wooden planks were edged with flickering light.

He lay flat on his stomach and put his eye to a gap between the planks. "It's the round room," he said with surprise. "I can see the purple flame."

Maxine stretched out beside him. "Such an awful, nasty secret," she murmured. "Upstairs the factory looks cold and empty, but it's all a lie. The basement's crawling with killers. The Hashashin can come and go through the graveyard, and the city never knows they're here."

"How many of them are there, do you figure?"

"Who knows? The place seems quiet now, though."

William crawled forward, keeping his eye just above the crack between the planks. "This could be our ticket."

"How do you mean?"

"I mean we might be able to find Grandpa without having to go down there and risk our necks."

Nura's eyes swept the darkened attic. "It is huge," she said. "It must cover the entire building below. We will have to look through many cracks."

They fanned out across the littered floor, treading softly.

"I can't see a thing over here," Maxine whispered. "The ceilings on this side have all been plastered over."

"Hey, M," said William. "Come have a look at this."

She trotted over, but as she reached the spot where William was standing, he caught her by the arm.

"Careful," he said, "that first step's a doozy."

Maxine looked down at her toes. The floor ended in an

abrupt edge that stretched away to either side of the factory. A black chasm lay below.

Nura joined them at the brink. "What lies down there in the darkness, do you suppose?" she asked.

"Beats me," William said uneasily.

"I guess we'll know when the sun comes up," said Maxine.

"Right. In the meantime, we might as well get some shut-eye."

"Honestly, Will. How can you even *think* about sleep at a time like this?"

"Sleep is pretty much all I can think about right now," said William, rummaging through an aisle of scattered trays and broken carts. He found a pile of discarded burlap sacks behind a sagging trough and flopped down with a groan. "We can figure out a plan in the morning, when it's light enough to see."

Maxine started to protest, then realized that she was bone-tired herself. "Well, maybe just a short nap," she said.

Nura joined them, and they settled themselves as best they could on the lumpy pile of sacks. A huddled dole of doves warbled softly in the rafters above, and through a broken bank of mullioned windows and a ragged hole in the roof, a thin gust of wind rustled in.

"What do you suppose our parents would say if they could see us now?" asked William.

"It's a good thing they can't," Maxine replied. "Mom especially. She doesn't need to know anything about it. She'd be worried to death." She tugged at a loose strand on the burlap sack beneath her. "I hope she's sitting on a beach somewhere, without a care in the world—her hair tied up in a scarf and a dozen nurses waiting on her hand and foot."

"She'll be all right, M," said William. "Everything will be just like it was before she got sick. You'll see."

Maxine sighed and hugged her knees to her chest. "She used to call me Blossom," she said, and William and Nura couldn't tell if she was talking to them anymore or just remembering aloud. "Like something small and pretty, you know? Something worth stopping to admire."

William let Maxine's words linger for a moment.

"What about you, Nura?" he asked. "You must be missing your folks, too, huh? I guess you must think about them all the time."

Nura didn't answer. She pulled the cigar box from her haversack and ran her finger along its edge, lost in reflection.

"I owe you both a great debt," she said. "You have placed yourselves in gravest danger for me—faced killers and entered darkened tombs—all to help me recover the mirror, when you could have left the city and returned to your grandfather's house. For all this and more, I offer my eternal friendship and my deepest thanks."

Maxine put her hand around the small girl's neck and pulled her close until their foreheads touched. "Well, gee, Nura," she said with a grin, "we accept your offer of eternal friendship. As far as I'm concerned, meeting you is the only redeeming thing about this whole wretched mess. I'd be awfully sorry if I hadn't."

Nura bent her head shyly. "I have no brother or sister," she said, struggling to find the words, "and unlike both of you, I have never known any cousin. But now we have found one another, and I am very happy. You are . . ." She faltered. "You are family to me," she said, clearing her throat and twisting the corner of her scarf.

William put his arm around her awkwardly and gave her shoulders a squeeze.

Nura's face broke into a grateful smile, and she looked as if she had just unburdened herself of a heavy load. She sat between the cousins, motionless for a while, deep in thought. Then she rubbed her eyes and yawned, and soon her head sagged against William's shoulder and her breath came in long, even intervals.

"Sweet dreams, kid," he said.

"She's not as fragile as she looks, is she?" said Maxine. "It's funny, but I think I feel the same way she does. Connected, I mean. I'm not sure why—we hardly know her at all."

"Oh, I wouldn't say that. We know her name, don't we? At least her first one."

"That's true." Maxine giggled. "Nura . . . It sounds funny, doesn't it?"

"It means 'light,'" said Nura without opening her eyes.

Maxine gasped and pinched her arm. "That's a nasty trick, you know, eavesdropping on your friends like that."

Nura laughed, for the first time since they had met her, perhaps, and then she closed her eyes again and recited softly:

"Ash-sha'b as-salik fi az-zolma absara nur 'azim."

"Is that your name? Your full name?" asked William. "It's kind of a mouthful."

She shook her head. "Ancient words. My parents chose them for me as a namesake. They speak of a people living in darkness and of a great light."

Nura's thoughts bent homeward, to days that lingered only in her memory: her mother, picking dates in the cool of the evening when the grove was fragrant with laurel and honeysuckle; her father, reading to her by firelight, his rough hand on her head where it lay in his lap.

"Ana . . . Baba . . . ," she whispered. "Where are you now? What has become of you?" She held the package close, as if it were a life preserver and she were floating in a vast ocean.

Maxine brushed the hair from the small girl's forehead and pulled her checkered scarf up under her chin. Nura smiled and scratched her nose, but her eyelids never lifted.

Above them the doves ruffled their feathers and settled on their perch. The night was cold now, and blighted. Maxine hugged her arms tight to her chest and stretched out on their makeshift mattress, wrinkling her nose at the disagreeable pong of mineral spirits and dusty hemp. She had never felt so lost and terribly afraid. These desolate thoughts were only in her head, of course, but Nura, on the edge of dreams, must have heard them all the same. She reached out and found Maxine's hand, and soon they both lay fast asleep.

CHAPTER 21

They awoke to shouts and the sounds of screeching
metal and groaning ropes. Morning had come and
gone, and the afternoon sun slanted in through the
dusty windows of the factory. William, Maxine, and Nura
rubbed their eyes and lifted their heads cautiously, remembering where they were.

"What's all the racket?" muttered William.

The sounds were coming from the direction of the pit.

They craned their necks to find the source, but their
view was obscured by a pair of enormous cast-iron boilers
that stood some ten feet beyond the precipice and rose from
the unseen depths toward the ceiling high above. The boilers had been invisible in the gloom the night before, but
now Nura and the cousins wondered how they could ever
have missed them. Their cylindrical surfaces were knobbed

with rivets and wheeled valves, and iron ladders were bolted to their sides.

Moving quietly, the trio crawled forward to a spot with a better view, flattened themselves to the floor, and peered over the brink.

Maxine exhaled weakly. "Heaven help us," she whispered.

They were looking out over an immense space. The room below had once been the main factory floor of the varnish works, but apart from a towering iron furnace on the far wall, the decaying equipment had all been carted out to make room for a kind of broad amphitheater. Black banners lined the walls, and the ever-present twelve-pointed star was painted large on the center of the floor. The room was teeming with Hashashin.

"They've turned the factory into some kind of temple," said William.

Down on the floor, in front of the unlit furnace, a wide wooden stage had been constructed, fronted with a broad flight of steps, and on this stretching dais there sat a great black chair, flanked by smaller versions of the same—six seats on either side.

A pair of *fida'i* turned a spoked windlass on one side of the room, straining against a system of ropes and pulleys that hoisted a spiked iron gate. When it was fully raised, the *fida'i* tied off the windlass and threw open a towering double door just beyond the iron teeth of the massive portcullis, and a pair of horses pulling a heavy cart clopped down a ramp outside. They passed beneath the spikes and came to a stop, stamping and snorting on the factory floor. A dozen of the Hashashin gathered around, and a long wooden crate was heaved down from the cart.

"That box looks awfully familiar," Maxine whispered.

The *fida'i* shouldered the crate and bore it up the steps like somber pallbearers, then laid it on the dais and crowded near.

There was a great stir around the box. One of the Hashashin brought a crowbar and bent over the crate, prying open the lid. The pack of *fida'i* gave a heave, and a shining black statue rose from the packing straw, towering over the cloaked men.

"Hey! They've got a jinni just like Grandpa's!" whispered William.

"That *is* Grandpa's jinni, blockhead," hissed Maxine. "They must have ransacked the manor."

The wooden figure was raised on a pedestal behind the great chair, its widespread legs straddling the throne while its menacing stare surveyed the temple.

"That's not all they've got," said William. "They must've found Grandpa's weapons case, too."

The *fida'i* rifled through the packing straw at the bottom of the crate, and now they held aloft the shining blades and the small clay spheres.

But at that instant every head in the temple turned as a door opened between the two boilers, directly beneath Nura and the cousins. A tall individual appeared, crossing the great hall and making his way to the dais.

The Rafiq mounted the steps and approached the

towering black silhouette. He climbed up onto the throne and stood on the seat, studying the statue thoughtfully for a moment, face to face, grasping the glass orb that hung round its neck and inserting it between the open jaws so that the gold chain draped from both sides of the creature's mouth like a bridle. The Rafiq's face creased in a sardonic smile, and he sat down in the large black chair and inspected the room, watching the preparations with satisfaction.

A group of gray-haired men entered, carrying small stools and enameled bowls with flashing instruments inside. They placed the stools beside the twelve chairs and arranged the bowls on top. Small bundles, wrapped in brown paper and tied with twine, were laid beneath the seats. An enormous bass drum stretched with animal hide was rolled up in front of the steps, and behind the dais the doors and vents of the furnace were opened wide and other servants brought wood and arranged it inside.

"It looks like they're getting ready for some kind of ceremony," said William.

Maxine elbowed Nura. "Are they going to wake the jinni?"

Nura shrugged, clueless.

"Something bad is getting set to happen, that's for sure," said William. "We've got to think of a plan to spring Grandpa, and the sooner the better."

"Shhh!" said Maxine. "He's headed this way!"

The Rafiq had risen from the black throne and was crossing the temple floor toward them. The children ducked their heads and cowered as he passed between the boilers and disappeared beneath them.

Nura pressed her eye to a crack in the floor and crawled away from the brink on all fours, following the same path that the Rafiq traveled below. She halted a short distance away, and Maxine and William crept to join her.

Through the narrow gap they discerned a new room: an opulent chamber with rich carpets and ottomans, filigreed screens, hanging lamps, and a splendid divan of blue and gold. The outline of the Rafiq passed beneath them as he crossed the floor and bent over a basin to splash his face, and they shrunk back as if, by some sorcery, he might see their hidden forms reflected in the surface of the water. He took up a towel and dabbed his eyes, then unbuckled the ivory breastplate from his shoulders and laid it to one side.

There was a knock outside the chamber, and the Rafiq opened the door to a young *fida'i*, who bowed stiffly and handed back the heavy ring of keys.

The Rafiq nodded and dismissed him. He returned to the far side of the room and took a black cigarillo from a lacquered box beside the divan. Grasping one of the pendant oil lamps, he swung it to his lips and lit the cigar in the flame.

Then, one by one, he snuffed the lights around the room. They heard the heavy clank of the key ring, followed by the closing of a lid or cabinet door, and then the long divan groaned as the Rafiq sank down upon it and sat motionless, like a spider in the dark.

The three children waited, spellbound, while only the fitful glow of the cigarillo served to show that the Rafiq remained. They might have lingered there forever if the deep peal of the bell in the round room had not echoed through the lair.

The Rafiq rose and relit the lamps and reassembled his vestments. He bent over the basin and washed once more and then departed from the room.

CHAPTER 22

A feast was laid out in the round room. The scent of lentils and warm bread, spiced cucumbers and roast lamb wafted through the slatted ceiling, drawing Nura and the cousins to the spot above the purple flame. They lay prone on the dusty planking, heads together, eyeballs pressed to the floor.

The bell rang again, and white-cloaked servants entered with pitchers, trays, and steaming platters. They arranged the dishes on the central serving table, and a long procession of *fida'i* filed into the room through the doorway marked with the emblem of the scorpion, seventy or eighty of them at least, removing their shoes and reclining on the cushions beside the low, curved tables that encircled the room.

When all was made ready, the Rafiq entered, and the

room fell silent. He made a slow circuit of the serving table, admiring the muraled wall and the sumptuous feast, and then he stepped toward the purple flame and stretched his hands wide as if waiting to receive an oracle from Alamut itself.

At length, he opened his mouth, but the words were unintelligible to William and Maxine, and they leaned close to Nura, who whispered the meaning in their ears.

"This is the night!" cried the Rafiq, turning as he spoke. "The night of triumph. An end to waiting. This is the eve of glory!"

Around the room the seated *fida'i* stiffened and bent forward.

"For every man, woman, and child upon these shores, it is the final night of ignorance and peace. Tonight they will lay their empty heads down to rest and dream their heedless dreams, but come the morning, they will wake to an unfamiliar dawn. Come the morning, they will know the yoke of bondage. They will know the meaning of fear. And come the morning, they will know the name of the Old Man of the Mountain."

"May his arm grow ever longer!" cried the *fida'i*, all as one.

"Tomorrow brings the daybreak of the Hashashin," continued the Rafiq above the din. "Tomorrow we blow a trumpet, for conquest and for power and for blood!"

The cries around the room swelled in a frenzy, and the Rafiq raised his hand.

"This city is the cornerstone of the West," he said. "But

the cornerstone will fall, and the tower will crumble. From their darkest slums to their marble mansions, every living soul will quail at the threat of the Hashashin. Every knee will bow at the foot of the one who sees all things in the Eye of Midnight, who declares the Unalterable Word, who holds the Key to Paradise.

"Twelve carefully chosen sacrifices," he continued, leaning forward and pressing his knuckles on the table. "Their princes and their tycoons, their gray-haired scholars and their strapping champions, their precious children and their cherished wives—tomorrow twelve of them will fall. Tomorrow, disguised as their own, we will darken their halls of power and their houses of worship, their markets and their homes, and they will fall like cattle beneath our blades. Twelve sacrifices with each new moon is all that it requires, and the rumor and dread of the Old Man of the Mountain will spread throughout this realm entire.

"And after, whenever the master commands them, they will tremble and obey. They will beg to do his bidding. We will plunder their treasure and rewrite their laws. We will carry their women and children away to Alamut to serve the whim of the Old Man of the Mountain. And all who will not bend the knee or pay a tribute of gold will pay a ransom of blood."

The Rafiq fell silent. His pupils narrowed to pinpricks, and he rocked where he stood.

"And blood will be shed within these walls as well," he murmured feverishly, nursing a lethal desire. "The Old Man's sworn enemy lies captive in our cells, and tonight his life is forfeit. We will observe the ritual, and he will answer for his trespasses."

"Grandpa!" whimpered Maxine.

"So may it be with all the enemies of the Old Man of the Mountain!" shouted the *fida'i*, raising their palms and hammering the tables.

"And now, a feast!" cried the Rafiq, clapping his hands. "In honor of the Old Man's triumph. Behold, his long arm giveth gifts as well."

A host of servants appeared and proceeded to wait on the seated *fida'i*. Up above, the floor creaked beneath the three children as they scrambled away in horror.

The Rafiq raised his heavy-lidded eyes to the ceiling, stroking his beard, and then he turned back to the feast.

The three children huddled among the long rectangles of late-afternoon sunlight that lay upon the attic's gray-planked floor, staring at one another with waxen faces.

"We've got to get out of here and tell somebody," whispered William.

"Who?" said Maxine. "Who will believe us? The police certainly didn't listen to us before—or to Nura, for that matter."

"There is only one way," said Nura. "We must find Colonel Battersea."

William nodded. "If we're going to do it, now's our chance."

"Our chance for what?" asked Maxine.

"Our chance to get those keys while everybody below us is stuffing their gullets."

"Brilliant," said Maxine with a scowl. "We'll march down there and say, 'Excuse me,' then waltz through the middle of their dinner party and barge straight into the Rafiq's bedroom."

"I have a better idea," said William. He led the girls back across the dusty attic to the precipice. "The Rafiq's private chamber is just below us, right? One way in is through the door in the round room, the one with the winged snake. But there's another entrance. We watched the Rafiq walk in and out of the temple right between the two boilers, so there must be a door straight below us. All we have to do is get down there and grab the keys before he finishes the feast."

"You're crazy, Will. Even if we do find the keys, we still don't know where they're keeping Grandpa."

"One can of worms at a time," he said.

"And how exactly do you plan to get down there?"

William pointed at the iron ladder fixed to the side of the boiler. "I'll go," he said. "You and Nura can stay here and be the lookouts."

"How are you going to get out there without splattering yourself on the floor?"

William peered across the gap between the precipice and the tall boilers, and his brow creased. He started to say something, but the words stuck in his throat.

"I know a way," said Nura. She disappeared for a moment among the rubble of the attic and returned dragging a discarded wooden plank, twelve feet long and half a foot wide. Struggling a bit, she and William heaved it out and rested the far end atop one of the ladder's iron rungs so that it spanned the fissure.

William gave the narrow footbridge a dubious look. He wiped the sweat from his palms and steadied himself with a hand on Maxine's shoulder, shuffling out tentatively onto the board. The plank bounced and sagged, and he gulped and clenched his eyelids tight.

"Open your eyes," Maxine said anxiously.

"I—I thought you were never supposed to look down," he stammered.

"Fine, so don't look down. But you can't cross a six-inch board with your eyes closed."

Shivering, William pried his lids apart one at a time.

"Well, go on," said Maxine.

"I—I can't. I told you back at the Needle, I'm scared to death of heights."

"*Vay canina*," muttered Nura in frustration. "This will never work."

They hauled William off the plank and away from the ledge, where he stood in a cold sweat. He wiped his brow with his sleeve and watched, incredulous, as Nura shifted her haversack on her shoulder, then stepped out onto the board and trotted lightly across the gap.

"While you're down there, have a look in the jinni's crate on the corner of the stage," he said. "See if you can find us something in there that might come in handy later."

Maxine shoved William to one side. "Never mind that.

Just get the keys and get back here. If you hear me whistle, forget the whole thing and make a run for it."

Nura nodded, and her head disappeared below the lip of the precipice.

Maxine shooed her cousin away toward the far reaches of the attic.

"Go keep an eye on dinner," she said.

William slunk back to their earlier vantage point above the purple flame. The feast continued in the round room below without interruption. Cups and plates clattered, the servers came and went, and the Rafiq sat apart from the *fida'i*, stripping the flesh from a pile of bones. William waved to Maxine across the attic and gave her the all-clear sign. She nodded and put her eye to the floor.

Beneath her Nura poked her head inside the door of the Rafiq's chamber, glancing about cautiously as she stole across the room and circled the wide divan. She opened a latticed cabinet against the wall, rifling through drawers and shelves, then turned and searched a heavy, carved desk and several wooden bowls atop a long black table.

Bending her head upward to the spot where she knew Maxine crouched and waited, she raised her hands in bewilderment.

"Get back here," Maxine hissed, but Nura was too far below to hear. The girl continued her fruitless search, and with each passing second Maxine's sense of impending doom increased. Her concentration was broken, though, by the sound of William calling to her from a distance.

"M!" His voice was low but urgent. "M, we're in big trouble." He jerked his head up from the floor.

Down in the round room the Rafiq had drained his cup and pushed aside his unfinished plate. Rising to his feet, he waited momentarily for a salute from the *fida'i*, then stalked out of the feast beneath the symbol of the winged serpent, back toward his chamber.

CHAPTER 23

William waved frantically across the attic. He stabbed his finger toward his feet and scrambled forward at a crouch, pacing himself with the Rafiq's progress below.

Maxine put her lips to the crack and whistled, but it was no good. Nura continued to potter about the room, oblivious to the approaching danger. She had just slumped down on the divan in frustration when something caught her eye. The polished corner of a small chest was visible beneath the cushions of the wide couch. She bent forward and her hand landed on the Rafiq's lacquered box. Her face flushed as she lifted the lid. There among a handful of cigarillos lay the heavy set of keys.

Nura glanced up toward the ceiling and waved the key ring in triumph, but to Maxine's great dismay she did not turn and head for the exit. Instead she pocketed the keys and made a slow circuit of the chamber, checking to see if there was anything she had missed.

Maxine's heart thudded inside her. William was nearly sprinting now, scuttering across the littered attic, and she knew that the Rafiq strode the same path below him. Her mind reeled, churning madly for some way to signal Nura.

"Your pockets, Will!" she cried as he slid up. "Empty your pockets!"

Blank-faced, William obeyed. He turned them both out, and the old coin left behind by the two visitors to Battersea Manor clattered onto the planks.

Desperately, Maxine snatched up the silver obolus and dropped it through the crack.

Nura whirled in surprise as the coin struck the ebony table with a ringing clank. Her eyes grew wide with startled comprehension, and she stumbled backward in a panic.

"Don't leave the coin behind, Nura," Maxine whispered to herself. "He'll find it."

But Nura's only thought was of escape. With a stricken gasp she lunged for the door, slipping out just as the Rafiq burst in on the far side of the room.

Maxine wilted with relief, and she and William turned and watched the top of the boiler ladder expectantly. Two minutes passed, and still Nura's head did not appear. William shifted from one foot to the other, and Maxine edged toward the precipice and gazed out over the darkened temple.

A single lamp burned upon the dais. In its feeble light she saw a furtive shadow stealing across the wide expanse below.

Nura mounted the steps of the dais and crept to the jinni's wooden crate. She lifted the lid and bent inside, tucking something into her haversack, then scampered back across the temple, back toward the boilers.

A few moments later her head appeared above the brink. William and Maxine pulled her eagerly off the bobbing plank. Too eagerly, perhaps, as the three of them all tumbled backward and landed on the floor in a heap. A clay sphere from the crate spilled out of Nura's haversack, landed with a dull thud, and rolled across the floor.

The cousins caught their breath and ducked their heads, but the sphere wobbled to a harmless stop.

"That was close," said William. "I thought we'd kicked over the lantern in the hay shed that time for sure."

"What is it?" asked Nura as she clambered to her feet.

"Grandpa called it some kind of fire bomb," William replied. "I don't think you want to be around when it breaks."

He fished the Rafiq's key ring from Nura's bag, along with one of the Hashashin daggers. "Nice job, kid," he said. The blade sang faintly as he drew it from the black sheath and tested the point against his thumb. "We gotta think of a nickname for you. Bulldog, maybe. Or Beartrap, or—"

Maxine flicked his earlobe. "You and your nicknames," she said. "Can we please just figure a way out of this place?"

"Aw, don't get yourself all in a twist," William said. "We got the keys, didn't we?"

"Yeah, well it's a little early to celebrate. They don't do us any good until we figure out where the Hashashin are keeping Grandpa."

"I'm still sorting that part out," said William. "We saw them drag Binny out of the round room, right? They took him through the doorway straight across from the storeroom, the one with the scorpion on it. If they're keeping Grandpa in the same place, then maybe we can find him from up here."

"I've been over to that side of the attic," Maxine said. "We can't see through the planks there. There's no way of knowing which room they've got him in."

"All right. Then I guess we'll just have to go down there and look for him. But we have to figure out how we're going to make it without being seen. The whole factory is crawling with Hashashin."

"Perhaps we should wait for midnight," said Nura. "When the lair is dark and everyone sleeps."

"There's no time," William insisted. "The Hashashin have something awful planned for Grandpa tonight. If we don't find him before then, it's bad news for sure."

Maxine nodded and pulled anxiously at her lip. "For Grandpa and this whole city," she said.

Twilight leaked in through the splintered hole in the roof. Beneath the attic's shattered ribs, Nura stood among a thousand broken shapes and prepared for one last labor, one final leg of her weary journey.

She removed the canvas haversack she had never been without, laying it aside. The black dagger she slid into her sleeve, and she fingered the blue *nazar*-bead on her necklace and tucked it beneath her collar. A brass lamp lay nearby, the same one she brought to the attic when they first arrived, and she took it up and checked the oil inside. When this was done, she found the battered cigar box once more and held it before her as if it were a sacred offering.

Nura untied the string slowly, and Maxine and William saw her hands tremble as she cast away the cigar box and lifted the Eye of Midnight. A spasm of doubt seemed to enfold her like a black shroud. She stood motionless before them.

"Take it," she said suddenly, forcing the silk-wrapped mirror into William's hands.

The cousins frowned at her in puzzlement.

"It's yours, Nura," replied William, pushing it back. "I don't want it."

"The mirror must be delivered to your grandfather, no matter what happens to me. Take it."

"There's no use talking like that, Nura. We're all in this together, and we're all going to make it out of here in one piece."

"You don't understand the strength of the Hashashin," said Nura in despair. "The Eye of Midnight must not fall into their hands. So many lives are at stake. The *fida'i* will strike terror into the hearts of the people of this country, and no one will be able to stand against them. And when a river of innocent blood has been shed in the streets and fear has spread like a fire of thorns, they will rule with ruthless cruelty, and the Old Man of the Mountain and his evil followers will trample every soul beneath their feet."

Her words were harsh and urgent, but her eyes were pleading.

"Keep the mirror, Nura," said William. "No matter what happens, we're not leaving you behind. When we find Grandpa, you can give it to him yourself."

Nura took back the small black bundle and hid it in a pocket of her dress.

"I have come so far for that chance," she said, wiping a tear from her cheek, "and now I fear that it will never happen."

"It's time," said William at last. "We've waited long enough."

Nura nodded. She searched the debris of the attic and found a small empty paint can and pierced it on a jutting nail.

"What are you doing?" asked Maxine.

"We must have something to conceal the flame," Nura replied.

They crept down to the storeroom, as silent as thieves, back between the crowded shelves and barrels, back to the round room, empty now, and they halted beside the undying violet fire as Nura lit her lamp and hid the flame beneath the can.

"That's where they took Binny," said Maxine, pointing across the room at the arched opening marked with the scorpion.

"It's a sure-enough hornet's nest in there," William said.

"That's where all the *fida'i* are camped out. Once we go through that door, there's no turning back."

The girls nodded, and they all took a deep breath, passing through the opening in a huddled knot. A few steps inside, they came to a locked door. Maxine and Nura looked over their shoulders tensely as William fumbled with the keys. At last the wards of the lock turned, and the door swung open.

Nura led the way into the dormitories of the *fida'i*.

Beyond the doorway the atmosphere of the lair was decidedly different. Every trace of luxury and opulence was gone. The walls were scarred and bare, and the passages were lined with a legion of cells—small, austere chambers with room only for a thin mattress and a single wooden chest.

Nura and the cousins crept single-file through the wandering catacomb, guided only by the weak glow of Nura's nail-pierced lantern, past a laundry filled with bundled garments and a darkened armory lined with blacksmith's tools.

Footsteps sounded ahead, where one passage met another. They pressed themselves against the wall and waited until the steps faded, then breathed again and continued on.

"Do you hear that?" whispered Maxine.

A chant rose somewhere in the dim halls ahead—a haunting murmur that surged and fell but never ceased. It grew louder as they went, until they reached the source. Ducking behind a tall urn on one side of the doorway, they knelt and beheld the appalling spectacle within.

The full muster of the *fida'i* was gathered in formation

throughout a wide hall. Crimson sashes were double-bound across their wraith-white robes, and unsheathed daggers darted in their hands. They moved with hypnotic precision, twisting and lunging as one, all the while intoning a terrible chorus, their voices swelling with the movements of their veering blades.

"What happened to their black cloaks?" whispered William.

"It looks like they're dressed for some kind of ceremony," Maxine said.

The three children shrank back, appalled to witness the full strength of Hashashin. Retreating from the training hall without a word, they fled deeper into the lair.

They went ahead in silence, treading softly and meeting no one, and came at last to a solitary wooden door, iron-banded and studded with black bolt-heads.

"In here," whispered William, tugging on the handle.

They slipped inside. No light shone in the corridor, and Nura risked unshielding her lamp. Halfway down the long hall, two doors faced each other, one on their right and one on their left, both sealed with heavy padlocks. Beyond them the passage stretched on farther into the darkness.

William chose the door on their left and tried several keys of likely size and shape. On his fourth attempt the tumblers surrendered with a tired groan. The shackle dropped, and they winced at the sound, waiting fearfully. Not a soul stirred in the darkness. They crept into the room, and Nura raised her lantern high.

And there, propped against the wall at the back of the

room, lay Binny. His ankle was chained to a rusted iron pipe, and his head slumped forward. He let out a groan and shuddered in his sleep, his chest rising and falling in rasping, uneven breaths.

"He looks bad," whispered Maxine. "He needs a doctor."

William swallowed uncomfortably. "First things first," he said. "We have to find Grandpa."

They backed out of the room and shut the door, and William crossed the corridor. He grasped the second padlock and tried the keys again.

"What's wrong?" whispered Maxine impatiently.

"I don't know," William muttered. "None of the keys seem to fit. I need more light."

Nura held her lamp close.

"Well, no wonder," he said. "There's something jammed inside the lock. It looks like the keyhole is full of wax."

"What?" cried Nura, backing away in alarm. "They know—" she stammered. "They know we have come!"

The children turned to flee, but the iron-bound door opened at the end of the hall, and a tall silhouette appeared, barring the way.

There was a sharp scrape, and a match flared.

"*Marhaba*," said the dark figure, cupping the flame and holding it close to his lips.

The keys slipped from William's hand and clattered to the floor.

There before them stood the Rafiq, his dreadful face lit by the orange glow of his cigarillo.

CHAPTER 24

"You've found my keys," said the Rafiq in impeccable English. "Many thanks. Let me offer you a reward for your troubles." He thumbed the obolus toward them, and the silver coin rolled to a stop at their feet. "I'm afraid I was forced to take some precautions with the lock, to ensure that no one disturbed my guest."

He looked the children up and down hungrily.

"How eager you all must be to see your grandfather again," he said. "Patience. You will join him soon enough. But first, I believe you have something that belongs to the Old Man of the Mountain."

His figure cast a monstrous shadow on the wall behind, and as he approached, his dark brows lowered and he cast aside all pretense of civility.

"The Eye of Midnight!" he demanded. "Give it to me!"

Nura and the cousins stood paralyzed, rooted to the ground. The Rafiq took a step toward them and caught William by the arm.

"Where is it?" he snarled, holding the end of his smoldering cigarillo close to the boy's cheek.

William felt the heat on his skin. He inhaled the stinging smoke and struggled wildly against the iron grasp.

"Let him go!" shouted Nura.

The Rafiq relaxed his grip and turned to face the girl directly. An evil smile flickered on his lips, and Nura's fingers went instinctively to the amulet at her throat.

"Do you think your *nazar* can save you?" he asked, backing her against the padlocked door. "Can it keep me from my prize, do you suppose?"

With a rattlesnake strike, he snatched the necklace and snapped the chain from Nura's neck. He held the blue bead in his palm and juggled it carelessly for a moment, then dashed it to pieces on the floor.

Nura let out a pitiful moan and dropped to her knees, scrambling to gather the scattered fragments. In despair she cast them all aside and covered her face with her hands.

The Rafiq laughed cruelly and pulled her to her feet. His nostrils flared, and his hand shot greedily into the bulging pocket of her dress.

"A thief, like your mother," he said with contempt as he withdrew the tightly wrapped bundle.

His face lit with a feral glint as he unwound the long ribbon of black silk and stroked the shining surface of the mirror. Muttering to himself, he read out the inscription in strange syllables that meant nothing to Maxine and William but made Nura cower against the cell door.

"It is an omen!" he cried fiendishly. "The Eye of Midnight is reclaimed on the night of the Old Man's glory! All just as it was determined and ordained long ago." He licked his lips and turned his back on the three children, gloating.

"Tonight you will bear witness to the victory of the Hashashin," he declared. "You will behold the ritual, and then you will be made a sacrifice."

He cradled the mirror, bare and flashing in his hands, as if he would call down lightning with it from above. And then suddenly he stopped, stirring from his exultation. He spun about savagely, and his triumphant leer twisted in a snarl of rage.

Nura's lamp lay discarded on the floor. The girl was no longer in the corridor.

The Rafiq smoldered, the cords in his neck bulging as he bellowed a command. Deftly he hid the Eye of Midnight beneath his breastplate just as a trio of the *fida'i* burst through the doorway with burning torches. The Rafiq pointed down the darkened corridor, and two of the men bolted away in search of the missing girl.

He watched them go and fumed. Then, turning a murderous glare toward the cousins, he shouted another command in his native tongue.

Silence fell around them, an interlude of uncanny stillness. In reply an echoing boom rolled throughout the lair— the mighty throb of a giant drum.

The Rafiq gestured toward the cell door, and the remaining *fida'i* held his torch close to the padlock until a stream of molten wax trickled out onto the floor. The Rafiq stooped to pick up the fallen keys, and he unlocked the door.

"Happy reunions," he said. With a vicious shove he sent the cousins sprawling into the cell.

The door slammed, and the padlock snapped shut behind them, sealing William and Maxine inside. The thudding drum continued in the darkness.

"Grandpa?" called out Maxine.

"Who—who is it?" came the hoarse reply. "Who's there?"

"Grandpa, are you all right?" she cried, crawling toward the voice.

"Maxine?" murmured the old colonel in disbelief. "Is that you?"

"It's me," she said, finding him in the gloom and laying her head on his chest. "Are you all right?"

"Yes, yes. Of course, my dear," he said. "Where is your cousin?"

"Over here," said William, groping toward the back of the cell.

"But what are the two of you doing here?" he asked, thunderstruck. He rubbed his eyes and shook his head, as if clearing his mind might dispel Maxine and William from the confines of the dank cell.

"Oh, Grandpa," said Maxine, her voice quavering.

"We kept your appointment," said William quietly. "We found the courier."

The old colonel's breathing halted briefly in the dark. "Where, my boy?"

"At the obelisk in Central Park."

Grandpa chuckled to himself. "Cleopatra's Needle . . . ," he murmured. "Yes, yes, of course." He leaned forward, and his chains rattled. "And the parcel?" he asked in a hushed voice.

"Oh, Grandpa," said Maxine again, "it was awful! The courier lost the package, and the gangsters who stole it caught us and tied us up, and there was a gunfight, and a tunnel underneath the graveyard, and we saw the Rafiq cut the White Rat's throat, and—" Tears came, and she couldn't continue.

Grandpa sat in silence, trying to make sense of her tangled story.

"Forgive me, both of you," he said, shaking his head. "I underestimated the danger grievously—perhaps disastrously. I would never have brought you to the city if I had known the stakes, not for all the relics of Solomon."

"It's real," said William. "The mirror—it's not just a bed-time story."

"No, my boy, it is not. The professors and the history books will tell you differently, of course. They claim that the mirror and the Hashashin are no more—gone the way of the dodo bird and the lady's corset. But that is only here in the West. Those who live among the Assassins know better."

"The Assassins? You mean the Hashashin?"

"Yes, the Hashashin. *Hashashin*, 'assassin,' . . . our English word is derived from the Arabic name bestowed upon these diabolical fiends. For centuries they have tyrannized the innocent inhabitants of the Orient, from the Great Pyramids to the Arabian Sea. And now they are here among us. Who knows how long they have been at their work, beneath my very nose, establishing their lair and tightening their stranglehold on the city."

"How many of them are there?" asked Maxine.

Grandpa shrugged. "In New York City? A couple hundred, maybe. Across the sea, perhaps a few thousand more. But never presume that the strength of the Hashashin relies upon their numbers.

"Horror is their chosen weapon. They have always used violence to exert influence, to move kings and topple seats of power. They disdain the vial of poison in the cup, the silent arrow from the battlement, the garrote in the dark. They are masters of disguise and assumed identity, virtuosos of death, and their instrument, their emblem, is the *djambia*—a ghastly, lethal blade—and the bloodier its work, the better, for with that steely brush and that scarlet stain they paint such a picture that none who witness it can ever forget."

Maxine tugged at the shackle that held Colonel Battersea's leg, and the chain rattled heavily on the concrete floor. "They have a plan for you, Grandpa," she said. "They mean to—to . . ."

"Let me guess: they intend to do me in," replied the old

colonel with a grunt. "Well, now, that's hardly a surprise. The Hashashin are not overly fond of me, my dear. My work has earned me more than a few enemies over the years, but the Old Man of the Mountain is my most formidable. And this is not the first time the two of us have locked horns."

"Grandpa, back at the train station," said William, "what happened?"

"I was shanghaied, my boy—ambushed on the platform, as you saw. They pushed me into a waiting automobile and etherized me. When I came to, I found myself here."

"Was it the Hashashin?"

"No, no. Garden-variety gangsters. The Old Man controls all the criminal organizations in the city now, it seems, bending them to his purposes."

"But why?" asked Maxine. "What does the Rafiq care about gangsters? Why does he even need them? We can't figure out why he didn't just send the *fida'i* to steal the mirror."

"The Hashashin will use any means necessary to spread their intimidation and influence," replied Grandpa. "But the Rafiq has another, more insidious reason, I suspect, for using these hired criminals.

"The *fida'i* have no knowledge that the Old Man of the Mountain has lost his mirror, you see. They believe that he is never without it. If the rank and file of the faithful were to learn that it is gone, his control over them would be unhinged.

"He caused a counterfeit to be made, which he keeps to fool his servants. Only a few of his inner circle—the Rafiq, for one—know the truth. But the Old Man lives always in dread of his ruse being discovered. As long as the true mirror remains beyond his grasp, he knows there is a danger that his secret will be found out and his power will be destroyed. He will not rest until the all-seeing mirror lies safe against his breast. And so the Rafiq labors mightily on his behalf to recover the mirror without revealing its presence to the faithful."

"Well, he got his way," said William despondently. "We had it, Grandpa! He snatched it from us in the hallway—right out of our hands. We were so close. We thought if we could bring it to you, then you might be able to stop the Hashashin's plans."

"Everything is ruined," said Maxine. "We failed you."

"Failed me, my dear?" Grandpa said in amazement. "Never in all the world. In fact, for all my foolishness, there is only one respect in which I was never wrong. My judgment of the two of you! A salute, *mes enfants*, to your resourcefulness and resolve. The old Battersea blood runs thick in both of you, sure enough. Born adventurers! To think that you actually managed to lay your hands on the Old Man's mirror!"

"Nura called it the Eye of Midnight," said Maxine, "the Key to Paradise."

"I have heard it called such things," Grandpa said. "Nura, though, is a name with which I am unfamiliar."

"We met her in the park," said William. "She's been with us ever since."

"Do you mean to say this girl is the courier?" asked Grandpa with surprise.

William nodded. "She's out there in the lair somewhere, all alone—if the *fida'i* haven't caught her already."

The colonel's jaw clenched and released mechanically as he contemplated their words.

"Grandpa, she's only twelve," said Maxine.

"I see," he said at last. "Well, let us hope the young lady shares some of your resourcefulness and resolve."

CHAPTER 25

The Rafiq's rant had echoed menacingly at the far end of the corridor as Nura crept away in the darkness. As she groped her way toward the end of the passage, her hand chanced upon a door handle. A moment later she found herself inside the empty temple.

Only the jinni saw her enter. She hesitated there in its sinister presence with a headful of helpless, haunted doubts. No longer did she hold out any real hope for her own escape. Her worries were for Maxine and William, and for Colonel Battersea and her parents; and still she clung to some indistinct notion of recovering the Eye of Midnight, no matter what the cost.

In the next instant, the enraged roar of the Rafiq reverberated in the corridor she had left behind, startling her from her tangled thoughts.

She scurried away along the back wall, behind the two

tall boilers and past the entrance to the Rafiq's chamber, where she had found the keys. Another wide doorway, framed with rough timbers, was just ahead. The dark opening exhaled a warm, animal scent, and she paused there uneasily. Gathering her courage, she tiptoed onward, but before she had reached the far side of the mysterious portal, two *fida'i* carrying torches burst out of the corridor behind her and stormed into the temple. They drew up short as they entered and cast their eyes across the wide expanse, scanning the length and breadth of the hall.

There was no time for deliberation. Nura dove through the dark opening, into an unswept room with low beams. A flickering lantern hung on a hook above her. She heard a snort and glanced about sharply.

At the back of the room a coal-black stallion and a dappled gray mare shifted in their stalls—the same pair of horses she had seen in the temple pulling the cart and the wooden crate. They nickered and pawed at her arrival, and Nura ducked under the wooden rail and stroked the mare's arched neck.

"*Hist!*" she whispered. "Hush, girl."

The mare quieted for a moment beneath her hand but suddenly shied again as the dreadful thump of a great bass drum echoed through the lair. Nura stood trembling, and the horses snorted restlessly. The drumbeat rolled again, and in a split second of unaccountable panic, Nura dropped to the ground and burrowed into the straw between the mare's hooves.

No sooner had she buried herself away than the *fida'i*

burst into the stable. Their torches swept the room, and the mare whinnied and stamped, her hooves thudding just beside Nura's head.

The men made a slow circuit of the room, then turned and hurried on.

Nura lifted her head cautiously from the straw and peered between the mare's forelegs. Outside the stable, preparations for the ceremony had already begun. Fire had been brought to the temple, and the doorway winked with amber light. The lair was alive now with the sounds of the Hashashin, and it was no longer safe for Nura to wander out into the open.

She rose and took a hurried inventory of the stable. A saddle and harness were slung beside her on the rail. She ran her hand over the smooth leather of the seat and cantle, measuring their curves with a practiced eye. A vague and desperate plan formed within her, and she set about saddling the mare.

"Grandpa, I thought you were retired," said William. "How did you ever get mixed up in all this?"

Colonel Battersea breathed a long sigh.

"Our time together has taken a turn I did not expect," he said at length, not answering the question directly. "I was convinced my adventuring days were behind me, I suppose. I had visions of a golden summer with my grandchildren, of reclaiming something, perhaps, that I had lost with my own children. But it seems now that my past has caught me up and would drag me in again, like quicksand."

A ponderous silence fell over the dank cell.

"Nura told us you could stop the Old Man's plans," said Maxine, and there was disappointment in her voice. "She thought you would know what to do. She said you were the city's only chance."

"A rather heavy burden for one person, don't you think?" said Grandpa. "The Rafiq's grand scheme may well succeed tonight, and I may not live to see the morning. But that will not be the end of the story. The Hashashin do not stand unopposed—they are not the only secret order in the wide world. There are others who keep watch."

"You mean to say there's more than one bunch of cutthroats roaming around the city?" asked William.

"Cutthroats? Not exactly. I refer to an invisible fraternity of guardians, sworn to a single sacred purpose. An order known as the Cafara—the Sons of the Cipher."

"And they're here—in New York City?"

"Sadly, no. The rise of the Hashashin on these shores was entirely unexpected, and the Cafara were not prepared to meet the threat with numbers of any significance. In fact, there were only three here. One of them is no more—a carpet merchant across the Brooklyn Bridge, murdered by the *fida'i*. A dear friend, and a great loss to me. The second I suspect you've met already."

"What?" said Maxine with surprise.

"Tell me," said Grandpa. "The man who delivered the

telegram to Battersea Manor—did he sport a long, ratty beard, like a Victorian poet?"

William nodded. "And he made a funny sign with his fingers. Like a circle over his heart."

"The Cipher," said Grandpa with a nod. "The cipher, or the zero, as you would call it, is the token of the order."

A light dawned on Maxine's face. "We saw zeroes all over Battersea Manor!" she said. "On the front bell and the mantelpiece, and on the door to the basement. Even on your letter opener."

"Yes, my dear. I am the third member, you see, of the contingent of the Cafara on this coast."

William squinted one eye. "Did you ever think of picking a different number than zero?" he asked. "Something a little more impressive?"

"Such as?"

"I don't know, like maybe seven, or thirteen, or something."

"Yes, well, the cipher is not exactly a number, is it? And it is rather impressive in its own way. It is naught—nothing. A thing of no apparent value. It is unseen and uncountable, a placeholder and a substitute. It is that which stands in the gap. And so it is with the Sons of the Cipher. The Cafara are an ancient order, comprising the descendants of the oldest Arab tribes—a chosen few who have taken a vow to protect the weak and the innocent and to stand throughout the ages against violence and oppression and a darkness that would spread across all the world."

"But you're not—" Maxine began.

"Not of Arab descent? No, my dear. I was made an honorary member of the Cafara many years back, during my years of service to the British Crown. I was adopted, you might say."

"Well, that explains it, I guess," said William.

"Explains what, my boy?"

"Explains why Nura thought you might be able to save the day. Her parents are prisoners of the Hashashin. She wanted to give you the mirror so that you could ransom them from the Old Man of the Mountain."

"Yes, well, that may be wishful thinking. The Old Man is not a generous negotiator."

"She seemed to think you'd be eager to help," said Maxine. "I thought maybe you knew them."

"The girl's parents?" Grandpa replied thickly. "Do I know them? Now, there's a proper question. I may have known them once. Once upon a time. I think I would very much like to meet this young friend of yours and ask her a few questions of my own."

Colonel Battersea leaned back against the wall, and his chains clanked faintly in the gloom. He scraped a knuckle across his whiskered chin and offered nothing more.

The drumbeat rolled on like the heartbeat of the lair. The cousins slumped against Grandpa and braced for what would come. For a long while no one spoke, and as the minutes passed, a disconsolate shadow settled over them and their spirits sank down, down, like stones tossed in a murky pool. Even Colonel Battersea seemed to succumb at last to the drum's relentless throb and the oppressive confinement of the bleak cell.

In the darkness he bowed his head and sighed. "What a fool I've been," he whispered to himself. "How did it ever come to this?"

Maxine laid her hand gently on his leg.

"I'm sorry, my dear," he said. "I thought you were asleep."

"Is there still hope, Grandpa?" she asked.

"Hope?" said Grandpa. "Yes, of course." He did his best to give her a reassuring smile, though he accomplished little in the dark.

"A popular poem comes to mind," he said, "about a sportsman named Casey—a cricket player, I believe. But it might well be applied to our current situation."

He rested his head against the wall, reciting slowly:

"The lane is long, someone has said, that never turns again,/ And Fate, though fickle, often gives a second chance to men."

"A second chance, huh?" said William, who had not been sleeping either, apparently. "Well, it better get here quick, or we're all in big trouble."

"There's something else, Grandpa," said Maxine. "They've got your jinni."

The colonel raised his eyebrows with mild interest. "Do they indeed?"

"Can they bring it to life, do you think?"

"I doubt that very highly, my dear." He chuckled. "The

Rafiq has heard the old legends, I'm sure. He would be exceedingly pleased to have a fiery jinni at his beck and call, but I suspect he has erected the *al-kaljin* more as a sort of trophy—a symbol of the Hashashin's dominion and power."

Maxine leaned her head on Grandpa's chest. "Maybe *we* could wake it up," she said dreamily. "Maybe it could help us get out of this horrid place."

Grandpa laid his chin on her head, indulging her fantasy. But in the darkness William tugged thoughtfully at his ear, repeating Maxine's words under his breath.

His thoughts were interrupted. Footsteps sounded in the hall outside. The *fida'i* were coming for them.

CHAPTER 26

A key turned in the padlock, and the *fida'i* entered. They dragged Grandpa and the cousins from the cell and pushed them into the corridor with Binny Benedetti, who staggered as he walked. The wrists of the two men were bound, and their captors herded them all into the temple, where the drumbeat thundered out across the open floor.

Blazing torches surrounded the empty hall, and the walls were draped with long black banners emblazoned with the symbol of the Hashashin. A fire had been kindled in the enormous furnace, and the inferno leapt hungrily inside, framing the dark shape of the jinni high above the center of the dais. Its long shadow stretched across the temple, and the statue flickered glossy black in the orange glow of the flames.

William and Maxine were separated and lashed to the pair of boilers at the very back of the temple—the thick ropes cinched tight around them until they could scarcely breathe—but Binny and Grandpa were brought to the center of the floor and made to kneel atop the great seal of the twelve-pointed star.

The Rafiq sat at the foot of the jinni, watching over all, his knuckled fingers gripping the armrests of the black throne like grasping talons. Behind him stood a man in a sleeveless bloodred cassock that brushed the floor. His scalp was smooth-shaven, the sockets of his eyes were smeared black with kohl, and he bore a great scimitar, which he shifted from one shoulder to the other as the prisoners were led into the temple.

All around Colonel Battersea and Binny, the floor of the factory began to fill with the phantom shapes of the pale-cloaked *fida'i,* and with gray-haired attendants, and with male and female servants, until the hall was awash with bodies and the room began to seethe in cadence with the drum. Then came other strains, strident and ecstatic, to join the steady throb. A group of pipers seated before the dais blew a droning dirge on flutes of bone, brass finger cymbals rang on unseen hands, and a high-pitched human wail rose above it all—a plaintive, frantic yodel that made the cousins' hearts beat hectically.

The tattoo of the drum quickened, and the music swelled, and the press of the faithful on the floor parted. A procession of twelve men approached the dais. They were dressed in hooded white robes girdled with crimson sashes, and their faces were grim as they ascended the steps and took their seats on either side of the black throne.

Twelve women carrying silver pitchers mounted the steps and stood before the twelve chairs, unwinding their headscarves and laying them across the knees of the seated men. They poured steaming water into the bowls at the feet of the *fida'i*, and, taking up straight razors and silver shears, they shaved the men's beards and trimmed their hair and mustaches neat, until the twelve sat freshly combed and clean-shaven and hardly recognizable from their former selves.

Gray-capped valets came forward next and undid the scarlet sashes of the twelve and removed their white robes, and the *fida'i* stood upon the stage, stripped of all but their linen undergarments. Finally the brown paper bundles under each chair were undone, and the contents were revealed.

Inside each was a different livery—disguises of various form and function. The *fida'i* donned these strange vestments, and Maxine and William looked no longer upon desert assassins but on inhabitants of the West.

Post carriers and milkmen; police officers and white-washers; bespectacled salesmen and collared priests—all standing in a solemn row.

The transformation was chilling and complete.

When all was accomplished, the Rafiq rose from his throne and walked the length of the dais, stopping behind each chair to mutter instructions of bloodshed and treachery, and then he held up his hand. The music fell silent, and he cried out in a loud voice for all to hear.

The meaning of the utterance was lost on William and Maxine, but in the frenzy of his rant and the wildness of his eyes, they felt his lust for destruction and power. The sound of the words drummed deliriously in their ears, rising in a feverish torrent, until at last he stopped and pointed a finger across the room, toward the iron gate and the city without.

"The hour has come," he called, and his voice rang like tempered steel. "The Old Man of the Mountain bids you rise and kill."

"We are living daggers," intoned the twelve *fida'i* as one, "thrust by the hand of the Old Man."

A great bellows was worked, and the flames in the furnace crackled ravenously and leapt within, so that even across the temple William and Maxine winced as they felt the heat on their faces. The drum began again, more urgent yet, and in the corner of the hall the windlass creaked, and the spiked portcullis began to rise. The faithful on the floor yammered and shook, their voices rising in an overwhelming clamor.

"Go!" shrieked the Rafiq above the din. "Go forth and destroy!"

The *fida'i* stirred and staggered, trancelike, from the dais, and William and Maxine watched in horror as they pushed through the grasping throng toward the open portal. At that moment, to the cousins' astonishment, the ropes that bound them fell slack. They shed the cords and turned to see Nura standing behind the boilers, her black dagger bare and flashing in her hand.

"Nura!" gasped Maxine. "Where have you been?"

The small girl didn't answer. Her eyes were focused

on the dais, where the Rafiq motioned to the bare-armed swordsman behind him. Raising his finger, he turned and pointed toward Binny and Grandpa at the center of the floor.

Nura stiffened and took a trembling step backward, as if she might turn and flee, but she mastered herself and faced the cousins once more.

"There is something I must tell you," she said, her words tumbling out in a frantic rush. She gave them both an earnest look. "You are my family," she said.

"Sure, Nura," replied William distractedly as he watched the scarlet-draped swordsman cross the dais. "You're like family to us, too."

"No," said Nura, shaking her head fiercely. "We are *family*. Flesh and blood." She pointed toward the kneeling form of Colonel Battersea. "Your grandfather is my grandfather, too," she said. "I was afraid to tell you. Afraid of what you might think. I imagined that you would look at the color of my skin and not believe the truth—that we are sharing the same blood, the same name."

She raised her hand, palm outward, fingers outstretched. Maxine stared at it in bewilderment, and then she raised her hand as well and nodded. For one moment, their palms met and their fingers locked.

A single tear slid down Nura's cheek.

"Remember," she said. "We belong to each other. Always." And with that she turned and darted away.

"Nura, wait!" cried William, but it was too late. He

started after her, but what he saw next made his knees go weak beneath him.

The swordsman descended the steps. He drew his scimitar as he crossed the floor, and when he had reached the prostrate forms of Grandpa and Binny, he spread his feet and raised the prodigious blade.

William and Maxine couldn't bear to watch. They clenched their eyes shut and abandoned every hope.

But in that hideous instant a great clatter filled the temple.

A pale horse thundered past the boilers, straight into the assembly of the *fida'i*, with Nura on its back. Its tail was high, its ears were pinned back flat, and its eyes rolled white as it slammed into the crush with a crunch of bone and sinew. Nura kicked the mare in the flanks, urging it deeper into the center of the crowd, and every soul in the temple turned to gaze at the unexpected entrance of the small girl and the ashen horse.

She never reached Colonel Battersea. Her hopeless charge fell short. In the midst of a hundred clawing hands, the mare reared and made an unearthly sound, and Nura tumbled from its back beside the twelve-pointed star.

Maxine screamed in horror as she watched the girl fall. At the center of the temple Nura floundered and tried to stand, but the *fida'i* swarmed over her in fury.

CHAPTER 27

Nura's arrival had thrown the Hashashin into howling disarray. Seizing his opportunity, Grandpa lunged to his feet, driving his shoulder into the midsection of the executioner. He swung his bound hands like a mallet, clubbing the man to his knees, and the curved sword clattered on the steps. In a single motion Grandpa scooped up the fallen blade and freed Binny's wrists and then his own. He pushed the gangster toward the open gate, and then, catching the terrified horse by the mane, he swung up on her back.

The mare bucked and launched her rear hooves, sending one of the *fida'i* sliding across the floor in a sodden pulp. Colonel Battersea posted in the saddle, settling the mare beneath him, and plunged her forward into the masses. His sword swept down along the horse's gray flanks, and the Hashashin fell away before him like spindrift breaking on a rocky shore. Cleaving a path to the bottom of the steps and sawing hard on the reins, he wheeled the horse to face the center of the dais.

The Rafiq's eyes burned with a smoldering rage, and he extended a long finger, pointing at Grandpa as if he meant to hold him frozen with the gesture. He spoke a word of contempt, and the faithful rallied to his call, swarming around Colonel Battersea like flies to a fresh carcass.

The pale horse shouldered through the throng of cloaked figures, her withers streaked with blood and sweat, and Grandpa slanted in the saddle and smote down the closing ranks behind. A single *fida'i* broke from the boiling mob and bounded to the end of the dais, taking a great flying leap off the top step and bowling Grandpa from the saddle onto the floor, but the old colonel rose and shrugged the enemy aside. All around him the Hashashin fell back before the sweeping scimitar.

Maxine and William watched their grandfather in awe. His years dropped away as he wheeled and slipped unscathed among the clutching masses. They had never seen anything as magnificent as the sight of the weathered knight in the gray flannel suit, his legs spread wide and his bright sword swinging in a savage compass—a shelter from the evil that assailed them.

But Colonel Battersea's heroic stand was doomed at last to falter.

"*Things fall apart,*" the poet Yeats once wrote, "*the center cannot hold,*" and in the end Grandpa staggered. At the back of the hall, the cousins watched helplessly as the horde of Hashashin pressed in around their grandfather.

"It's now or never," William whispered to his cousin, glancing anxiously toward the top of the boiler. "We have to try to wake the jinni."

He had no time to explain. Pushing Maxine aside, he seized the boiler ladder and had just begun to climb when he felt a crushing weight on his back. He lost his grip, and his forehead struck the iron rung with a clang. He fell from the ladder and crumpled on the floor.

A rough hand rolled him over, and a heavy knee sank down on his chest. William groaned in pain.

One of the white-cloaked *fida'i* knelt over him and drew his knife. With a jerk he forced the boy's chin up and raised the glinting blade, his knuckles white upon the hilt.

"You have troubled the Old Man and defied his servants," he said, his voice as cold and dead as the plague. "Your life is forfeit."

William looked up at the snarling face and was stunned to see Maxine's own pale features hovering there as well, just behind the man's right shoulder. Her lips tightened in a thin line of determination, and in the next instant the Hashashin gave an inhuman howl, flailing his arms and grasping at the middle of his back. William watched in confusion as he lurched and twisted, and then he glimpsed a glint of crimson and understood. There between the man's shoulder blades was Maxine's ruby hat pin, quivering like an arrow.

The *fida'i* reeled away, and in the brief space that Maxine had bought him, William struggled to stand, then scrambled up the ladder once more, his feet missing the rungs in his panic as the living, surging floor fell away beneath him. His palms were wet, and his head swam. Looking down, he saw Maxine's tense face following him as he climbed.

He reached the top of the ladder and eyed the narrow plank. His legs felt like limp asparagus as he edged out onto it, out to the middle of the gap. The board bobbed woozily under his feet, then gave an ominous crack.

In a fit of desperation William lunged for the far side of the gap, and as he did, the timber splintered and fell into the void. He felt a searing throb in his chest as he crashed against the far wall and clutched madly at the rough planking. For a moment only his chin was visible above the brink, and then, with a supreme effort, he hoisted himself up over the edge, laboring to pull himself onto the attic floor.

He lay there, gasping and weak, uncertain that he was still alive. The clay sphere sat beside him on Nura's canvas sack. Grasping it and clambering to his feet, he turned his gaze out across the temple and spotted the black statue.

There was no time to think of the cost of missing his aim. Down below the *fida'i* had pinned Grandpa in the middle of the floor, and the Rafiq was descending the steps toward him. William took two short steps and let the clay sphere go, launching it with all his strength. It arced unseen among the gloomy rafters of the temple, and then a thunderous boom echoed across the hall. Behind the Rafiq, a blaze flared, furious and brilliant, at the foot of the jinni.

The statue made a savage roar as the explosion engulfed

it. Blue flames licked over it, and the black-lacquered surface blistered like the pox. The creature's horsehair beard crackled and curled about its head, and the jinni seemed to shrug and rise up to its full height within the pyre. Its eyes burned white. Vivid tongues wormed from the gaping mouth, and it stood like a diabolus, wreathed in a column of twisting fire. The black pennants that draped the furnace ignited with a hungry growl, and the flames raced high toward the ceiling. The Rafiq reeled as the temple kindled behind him, and in the choking reek of black smoke the multitude on the floor descended into chaos.

Moments before, the full wrath of the Hashashin had been fixed on Colonel Battersea, but now the ranks of the faithful parted and dissolved. They fell back from the dais and scattered like the whirling sparks above, driven on a fiery breeze.

CHAPTER 28

William peered down over the brink. Maxine ran in crooked circles below, her face reflecting the fitful flames as she searched the hall frantically for Nura. William's mind spun as he tried to work out some way to reach the temple floor. The wooden plank was gone now, and the ladder loomed a million miles away. He thought of the stairway at the far end of the attic, but there was no time to retreat through the storeroom and circle back.

Without giving himself time to reconsider, he took a running leap for the boiler, flailing through the air. He grasped at one of the iron rungs, and the metal shrieked as his hand closed tight around it and the bolts that held the ladder to the side of the boiler broke loose. The frame swung free, and for a heaving moment William hung limp in empty space, dangling like a rag doll over the floor far below, but the ladder swayed back, returning to vertical, and his scrambling feet found the rungs.

The fire was raging now. The flames climbed the walls of the factory and scuttled crab-wise across the ceiling. On the steps of the dais the Rafiq raised his hands in outrage as he marshaled the twelve assassins and drove them toward the open gate. A tremendous roar filled the temple, and in the midst of the bedlam and black smoke the *fida'i* trampled everything in their path as they groped for Colonel Battersea in a blind fury.

William reached the ground and stumbled to Maxine's side, and they stared in amazement as they looked out across the temple.

In the midst of the blaze Binny was on his feet. He held his left arm against his side as he staggered forward, crossing the crowded floor like an apparition. His shoulders were stooped, and his coat was soaked with blood, but he walked an unswerving path toward the Rafiq, and his eyes blazed as he grasped the Hashashin from behind and turned him around.

The Rafiq looked at him and sneered. "Son of a dog," he spat, squaring his shoulders and raising his chin. "It seems your foolishness knows no bounds. Is this temple truly lacking for dark corners where you may go and die?"

"I told you before," rasped Binny, "I won't be pushed. You're a blight on this city—an oozing sore."

He raised his arm to strike the Rafiq, but the Hashashin caught his wrist and grinned monstrously. Drawing close, he laid his hand on Binny's neck and pressed his thumb into the gangster's open wound.

Binny withered in pain. His head sagged onto the Hashashin's shoulder, and the Rafiq whispered in his ear words of devastation and despair. With a gloating grin, the Hashashin stepped back, and his hand dropped to his dagger.

And then the arrogance in the Rafiq's countenance wavered, replaced by a sudden spasm of doubt. He glanced down at his waist.

His jeweled scabbard was empty.

Lifting his eyes in bewilderment, he saw the gangster swaying before him and beheld his own flashing dagger clenched tight in Binny's hand.

The Hashashin howled with rage and took a step backward, but Binny seized him by the beard. Summoning the last of his dying strength, he buried the dagger in the Rafiq's chest.

The Rafiq tried to speak. He laid his hand on the jeweled hilt jutting just below his collarbone and strained to pull it free, but the blade was stuck fast. With a final twitch of his eye, he slewed sideways on the stairs, falling at the feet of the gangster.

Binny sank down on the steps. He sat motionless, like a man bent in silent prayer, and then he toppled forward and did not rise again.

The faithful in the temple halted where they stood. Their clamoring ceased, and they stared at their fallen leader.

Maxine and William skirted the frozen multitude and

mounted the steps of the dais, kneeling beside the body of the Rafiq. His white mantle lay open, and Maxine pushed aside his ivory breastplate, revealing the hidden treasure beneath. With a tug on the black silk sash, she pulled free the Eye of Midnight.

Maxine climbed boldly to the top step, the mirror dangling in her hand. Her hair streamed wildly about her face. She turned and looked out over the temple and raised the Eye aloft.

The *fida'i* fell back. They stared at the flashing mirror in dismay, then turned, stumbling, and fled the temple in every direction.

Blazing timbers rained down from above, and the heat from the fire was unbearable. The temple was coming all apart. The hall burned like the mouth of hell, and William and Maxine stood in the midst of the churning black smoke, searching the floor for Nura. High atop its charred pedestal, the corrupted form of the jinni fractured at the knees and tumbled backward off the dais.

Breaking through the scattering mob, Grandpa bounded up the steps. He took William and Maxine by the arms and dragged them headlong toward the open gate.

"Grandpa, no!" screamed Maxine. "We can't leave Nura!" But her words were lost in the awful din, and Colonel Battersea pulled them relentlessly on.

They had almost reached the gate when Grandpa paused and turned, glancing back into the depths of the burning factory.

Through the billowing smoke, the scarlet swordsman

and a remnant of the *fida'i* pursued. They paid no heed to the fire, and their long, curved daggers were unsheathed.

Colonel Battersea shoved his grandchildren out beneath the teeth of the iron portcullis, but William stumbled just beyond the gate. Maxine clutched at his arm and pulled him to his feet.

Looking back in despair, the cousins saw Grandpa make his stand beside the spoked wheel. He raised his broken sword and swiped in two the rope that held the iron bars aloft. With an anguished cry, he dove out of the temple, and the spiked gate fell like a guillotine behind him, pounding the floor with a ringing boom.

The executioner and the merciless *fida'i* stood for a moment at the iron bars and seethed; then, glancing toward the burning roof, they turned and retreated through the temple.

Maxine and William followed Grandpa up a long incline, their seared lungs heaving as they staggered to safety and gulped the unspoiled air. Lifting their eyes toward the city, they blinked insensibly in the morning light, as if they had forgotten the living world outside.

CHAPTER 29

The *New York Champion* left Penn Station at precisely twenty-eight minutes past eight in the morning. Even after it lurched to life, Maxine and William cowered in their seats, and the train clattered on for some time before they began to believe that the danger had really passed.

Neither of them stirred as the train left the city and started its long curve down the coast. The morning sun broke above the skyline in the east, and, looking back, Maxine and William began to shed great silent tears. They wept for weariness and fear, but most of all they wept for Nura. Finally they cried themselves to sleep and slumbered like the dead.

Grandpa prodded them as the engine pulled into Hendon Station, and the cousins managed to clear their heads and scramble out before the doors were closed. Behind them the old colonel winced as he stepped down stiffly from the train.

"Grandpa, you're hurt!" cried Maxine, spotting a scarlet stain beneath his tattered jacket.

"No, my dear. It's nothing. Just another scar for the collection."

The cousins followed Grandpa along the tracks toward the clapboard station house. "Excuse me for a moment," said the colonel, stopping at a phone booth just outside the station door. "There's a call that should be made before we get the car. I must pass on word of last night's events."

Grandpa stepped inside, and Maxine and William were left alone.

The platform was empty. A songbird chirruped in the trees nearby, and the station shingle creaked a little in the breeze. Maxine glanced at a livid welt on William's grubby cheek and the goose egg on his forehead.

"How's your face?" she asked.

"All right, I guess," he said with a shrug.

"Yeah, well, it's *killing* me."

"Oh, that's rich. Yours ain't so lily white either, you know," replied William. "And I hate to break it to you, but it looks like the ol' freckles are still multiplying."

"*Ain't*'s not a real word," said Maxine, "and you're just jealous."

William chuckled a little, just for a moment, and then his smile dimmed.

"It's over, isn't it?" he asked heavily.

Maxine nodded and stared down at her shoes, tucking a loose strand of hair behind her ear.

It seemed unreal, somehow, that they had come so very

far, weathered every storm, only to end up on the platform back in sleepy old Hendon.

"What happened to your hat?" asked William.

Maxine gasped and reached for her head.

"I don't know," she said, crestfallen. "I must have dropped it somewhere."

"No kidding? That hat belonged to your mom, didn't it? You probably should have taken better care of it."

Maxine's eyelid twitched, and she fixed William with a vinegarish look. "Remind me of that the next time I get some crazy idea in my head about saving your life," she said. "It might have stayed on better if I hadn't lost my hat pin."

"Oh yeah, your hat pin. I guess you did kinda save my life, come to think of it," he said. "You know, M, I have to admit . . . you make a pretty good sidekick."

"Sidekick?" she replied, and she gave him a shove toward the tracks.

"Aw, come on. Can't you take a joke? Look, I've got a present for you." He dug his hand into his coat pocket and pulled out the old red hat.

"Will!" she cried, staring at it wide-eyed. "Where did you find it?"

"I picked it up on the steps of the temple."

Maxine ran a finger along the inside of the hat and found the old photo of the unknown boy standing in front of Battersea Manor.

At that moment Grandpa stepped out of the phone booth and motioned toward the station house.

"Ten-hut, you two," he said.

Maxine tucked the photo away again and pulled the hat down firmly on her head as they followed Grandpa into the station house.

"Thanks, Will," she whispered. "Really."

"Don't mention it," he said with a wink. "It's the least I can do for the girl who saved my life."

Outside the station house and around the corner, they found Grandpa's Rolls-Royce Phantom parked behind the grocer's, and they piled inside.

"Now," said the old colonel, glancing back at the cousins from the driver's seat, "perhaps we might—"

"Don't you want to see it, Grandpa?" interrupted William, giving Maxine an elbow.

Maxine reached inside her coat and found the Eye of Midnight, presenting it with ceremony to Grandpa. His bushy eyebrows snapped to attention, and he frowned as he took it.

A low whistle escaped his lips as he examined the gleaming disk, testing its weight in his hand. "I've never seen it before, did you know?" he murmured, tracing the etched surface with his fingertips. He was lost in thought for a moment, and then he slapped his knee.

"Amazing!" he said aloud, and the cousins craned their necks to see what it was he found so remarkable.

"Oh, not this!" he said. "I mean you two!" He tossed

the mirror on the passenger seat and coaxed the Phantom's engine to life, and with that the silver car sped away.

"You're rather extraordinary, you know," said Grandpa. "Alone there in my dark cell I brooded endlessly over what had become of you. I could only pray that you had escaped the city unharmed. And then, astoundingly, against all odds, you appear out of nowhere, with a trophy—the Old Man's coveted treasure!"

William grinned. "It raised quite a ruckus, didn't it? When M held the mirror up in front of the temple?"

"Rather. The *fida'i* found the sight of it thoroughly confounding, I believe," said Grandpa. "As I told you before, the faithful are under the delusion that the Eye of Midnight is the wellspring of the Old Man's power and that he is never without it. Maxine's exposé of that deception has torpedoed his grand conspiracy at a stroke. It will take the old jackal some time to tidy up the damage, and the Cafara are no longer ignorant of his schemes. If he tries again, the Sons of the Cipher will be ready to meet the threat."

A sudden lurch of the Phantom brought their focus back to the present, and the cousins realized that they had left Hendon behind and were traveling in haste.

"This isn't the way back to the manor," said Maxine.

Grandpa glanced back at his two grandchildren. Their eyes were red-rimmed, their faces streaked with grime. The knot on William's forehead shone like a traffic signal.

"You look as though you could use a meal and a bath. I daresay you've earned them, and you shall have both. But in light of the past nights' proceedings, I'm afraid we cannot return to Battersea Manor. We must leave home behind for the time being."

"Where are we going?" asked William.

"Back to the city," said Grandpa with a watchful glance through the rear window, "though not directly and not for long. Tonight we'll stay in a remote spot along the way, someplace with a hot meal and a soft bed. And then tomorrow—"

"Tomorrow?" said Maxine.

"Yes, well, we can talk about tomorrow later."

They arrived at last at an old wayside lodge beside a secluded lake. The Mayfly Inn showed the wear of many long seasons and sagged now beneath the weight of a comfortable shabbiness. A tired yellow dog in charge of greeting guests limped over to them, tail wagging, and licked their hands.

"I expected you earlier," said a man sitting on the front steps with his face buried in a newspaper. He lowered it as they approached, folding it carefully, and the cousins recognized his matted beard in an instant. It was the man who had delivered the telegram to Battersea Manor.

"We took the long route, as a precaution," said Grandpa.

The man stood and made the sign of the zero over his heart with his thumb and forefinger.

"Nothing will prevail," he said.

"The Cipher does not sleep," replied Colonel Battersea, returning the salute.

The man produced a black revolver and handed it over discreetly. "I thought you might be wanting a replacement for your Webley," he said with an easy smile. "Try not to lose it this time."

Maxine tugged on her grandfather's sleeve. "Grandpa," she said, whispering behind her hand, "who *is* he?"

"Pardon me, my dear," he replied. "Sufjin, let me introduce you to my grandchildren—Maxine Campbell and William Battersea."

"*Tasharrafna*," said the man, addressing the cousins with a low bow. "I believe we met once before. If the story the colonel has told me on the telephone is to be believed, the Sons of the Cipher owe you both a debt of gratitude."

The cousins blushed, suddenly bashful.

"Sufjin is an old friend," said Grandpa. "Saved my life on more than one occasion and won't let me forget it, the scoundrel."

"Ah, *effendi*," said the Cafara, "your gray head would forget your own name if you did not have me to remind you."

That evening Sufjin joined the Battersea family for supper on the back porch of the inn, overlooking the lake. The widow who owned the lodge, a woman who had long ago lost her sense of humor but not her prodigious sense of hospitality, brought fried catfish and corn bread and buttered turnips and beans with bacon until William and Maxine were set to burst, and then, on top of all the rest, she brought a banana cream pie, and they found room for that, too.

At last, tipping his chair back from the table, Grandpa looked squarely at the cousins. "Now that you've been sufficiently reprovisioned," he said, casually plying his molars with a toothpick, "perhaps we might hear about your adventures in a bit more detail."

And so they told it all, start to finish—Cleopatra's Needle and their encounter with Nura under the bushes, and the shoot-out in Binny Benedetti's hideout, and the begoggled Pigeon, and the theft of the Rafiq's keys. And if in the telling the cousins painted themselves in a slightly pluckier, more intrepid light than they had displayed in the midst of it all, then perhaps they might be forgiven—the experience had already begun to assume a romantic luster in their imaginations even as the events faded into memory.

Sufjin and Colonel Battersea listened with inscrutable expressions, only periodically remembering to blink, until Maxine and William paused at last. Grandpa shook his head and let out a chuckle that swelled into a deep, ringing guffaw.

"What a fool I've been!" he said. "Sending you to dodge bullets and wander about in darkened cemeteries. It seems you've squeezed more peril into the last three days than most people manage in a lifetime. Are you sure you didn't leave anything out?"

"There is one thing," said William. "The brawl in the

temple. I've never seen anything like it. You were amazing. You didn't tell us you knew how to handle a sword like that."

Grandpa chuckled and gave him a wink. "I did say I had a few secrets, didn't I?"

He gingerly lifted his arm, which was bandaged now and wrapped in a sling. "The truth is, I'm getting old, my boy," he said. "Past my prime. The spirit is willing, but the flesh is weak."

"Do not believe a word of it," said Sufjin. "Where I am from, we say, 'Old dogs know the most tricks'—and you will find that your grandfather has learned more than a few over the years. He is as stubborn as a donkey, most assuredly, but a little smarter, and there is no one you would rather have at your side when you are in a scrape.

"Beyond that," he added, looking over the old colonel's ragged appearance, "Horatius Battersea is the only man I know capable of holding off a temple full of Hashashin in dress shoes and a flannel suit."

CHAPTER 30

The sun was buried now behind the horizon, and the still lake was a perfect mirror beneath a dark crown of trees silhouetted against the day's last light. The two men and the two young cousins sat with full stomachs and heavy thoughts, while up in the eaves of the porch a gray spider slipped down a thread of silk and dangled above them, twisting slowly. No one spoke, but they all lifted their eyes, and as they watched, the spider began to spin.

Cobwebs are a common enough thing, of course, found in barns and tree branches and dusty attics everywhere, but the making—the web craft—is a mostly private affair, seldom witnessed and often overlooked. On this evening, however, four pairs of eyes watched, transfixed, as the spider went about her work.

She moved with grace and dexterity against the bluing sky, never hesitating, never perplexed by any riddle of engineering or architecture, as she crossed and recrossed her handiwork, tracing a memory.

"Who taught you how, little one?" murmured Grandpa as he watched. "When did God whisper the steps in your ear?"

Beside him Maxine stirred. Balling her fists, she snatched a napkin from the table and swept the web away.

"Hey, what'd you do that for?" said William.

Grandpa sat forward in his chair and frowned. "I was wondering the same thing."

Maxine sniffed and turned her back on them. "What's the difference?" she snapped. "It was just an ugly old spider."

"I thought it was rather charming," said Sufjin, but Maxine was too distraught to hear.

"Grandpa, you don't really believe God cares about spiders, do you?" she said, looking back at him with a kind of hopeless desperation.

"Maxine, come here," he said, and she went to him and he held her. "What is it, my dear?"

The tears came suddenly, and between her sobs she blurted out, "Why did it have to be Nura? When I saw her fall from the horse, I begged for God to save her."

Grandpa sighed, comprehending now, fathoming her emotion, but he hugged her close and let her cry.

"I understand, my dear," he said. "I know something of loss myself."

"We promised Nura we wouldn't leave without her," Maxine said. "But in the end we just let her go. We didn't do a thing to save her."

"There are circumstances in life beyond our control, Maxine. Monsters that we never knew existed. What happened to Nura was not your fault."

But Maxine shook her head with a sob. "No," she said. "We left her there alone, and now we've lost her."

"You haven't lost her, Blossom," said Grandpa. "You carry her in your heart."

Maxine glanced up at him, taken aback. "Why—why did you call me that?" she asked.

"I'm sorry, my dear. It's a name I used to call your mother when she was very small. An old habit, I suppose."

"It's all right," she said. "Now I know where she got it. For just a second it felt like she was here."

Grandpa nodded and took her hand in his. "The answer to your question is yes, my dear," he said. "Yes, God cares about spiders, and sparrows . . . and he cares about Nura. It is too early to give up on the young girl, I believe. While hope remains, hold fast."

Maxine sniffled and wiped her eyes, and her expression changed.

"She's not just any young girl, is she, Grandpa?"

Colonel Battersea hesitated, reading his granddaughter's face. "No, my dear. She's not," he said at last. "Why do you ask?"

"Just before she left us, she said, 'You are my family.' She called us flesh and blood."

"She wasn't talking sense," William said. "She was practically hysterical."

"Hysterical?" replied Grandpa. "Perhaps. Though I believe you know perfectly well she spoke the truth."

Maxine shook her head. "But how? How can it be?" she stammered. "She talks with an accent, and her skin is dark—"

"Surely you're not basing your judgment on the color of her skin? It has nothing to say about the question. It's neither here nor there."

"More riddles," said William with frustration.

Grandpa nodded wearily. "As the two of you are learning, I have many secrets," he replied. "Not all of them are entirely admirable."

He paused, as if he needed to work up the courage for what came next. Sufjin looked away uncomfortably, and Grandpa continued:

"Your parents—your mother, Maxine, and William, your father—they are not my only children. I have an older son, whom I have not seen these twenty years and more. The last I knew, he was living somewhere in Turkey or Syria, with a wife of Eastern descent."

Maxine backed away from Grandpa and slumped in her chair, her head swimming, and William squinted as if he were working out a difficult sum. "So that means . . . ," he said, "that means Nura—"

"Nura is our cousin," Maxine murmured, "your granddaughter."

"Yes," said Grandpa. "Though I assure you I knew nothing of her existence until last night."

Maxine took off her mother's hat and found the yellowed photo of the teenage boy with the suitcase, standing on the steps of Battersea Manor. She handed it to Grandpa.

"Where did you get this?" he asked, startled.

"I found it in the nursery closet, back at the mansion."

Grandpa stared at the photo, deeply affected. "This was my son," he said at last. "Your uncle David."

"But our parents never even mentioned him," said William with a puzzled expression.

"No, I'm not surprised."

" 'Keep the secret, never tell . . . ,' " Maxine muttered, her thoughts returning to the echoing hallways of Battersea Manor.

"Eh, what's that?" asked Grandpa.

"I don't know, really," she answered. "Just something I saw scratched inside the closet where I found the photo. 'Keep the secret, never tell, unless you want your throat to swell.' "

Grandpa's shoulders sagged as if the scrap of rhyme had saddled him with a heavy burden.

"My son and I had a falling-out, as fathers and sons sometimes do. He ran away and swore never to return. From that day forward I did not permit David's name to be mentioned in our house. It was a tyrannical thing to do, but then again, playing the tyrant was not an entirely unknown role to me."

"You made them pretend he never existed?" exclaimed Maxine. "How horrible!"

"Horrible?" said Grandpa. "Yes, I suppose that's true

enough. My bitterness was not your mother's, Maxine, or your father's, William, but I managed to force my own misery upon them. Their brother's memory became a dark secret, the stuff of superstition and sinister nursery rhymes."

"Well, I guess when they were all grown up and out of your house, they could have talked about him," William said.

"Sometimes the burdens we lay on others' shoulders remain long after they are free to drop them, my boy. I'm afraid that is your parents' case. I hope a day will come when they might forgive their stubborn father and speak openly of David and remember him fondly."

Grandpa eyed his bewildered grandchildren, and his brow was creased and careworn.

"Beyond that," he said, "I hope against hope that a day will come when they may look upon his face again. If it is in my power, I would see it happen."

CHAPTER 31

The cousins settled into soft pillows that night, under clean, cool sheets and chenille spreads, but before sleep took them, Grandpa entered the room. He set the Eye of Midnight on the nightstand and pulled a chair between their beds.

"The time has come to talk about what happens next," he said. "I find myself, as the saying goes, on the horns of a dilemma. The fact is, we cannot stay here, any of us, as we are all in grave danger.

"Thanks to the two of you, and to Nura, the threat of the Hashashin on these shores is crippled now. The Rafiq is dead, and the *fida'i* are scattered; the hidden lair is reduced to a charred ruin, and the Old Man's sinister plot lies in shambles. But even though the danger to the city has passed, our own peril is still very real. Our enemy knows that we possess the mirror he covets, and now he grows desperate, and his killers will no longer proceed with caution. The Old Man will send more of his *fida'i*, and he will strike down anyone who stands between him and his treasure, though he risks much in doing so in a far land of whose customs and laws he knows little."

"So what can we do?" Maxine asked bleakly.

Grandpa hesitated. "I intend to return the Eye of Midnight to the Old Man," he said.

"What?" cried William.

"After all that?" said Maxine. "After everything we've been through? You'd just hand it over to the Hashashin without a fight?"

"Hand it over? Not exactly. I plan to take it to the Old Man in person. I will go to his fortress in the desert and bring his precious trophy to him. It is of no worth to me, but he has something there that I value very much."

"Uncle David," said William.

Grandpa nodded gravely. "The Old Man's fortress is far from here, across three seas," he said. "Two of water, one of sand. It will be heavy work."

"And what will you do with us?" asked Maxine.

"I haven't decided," said Grandpa slowly. "I could put you on a train back to your homes tomorrow. You could stay with neighbors, perhaps." His eyes dropped and he smoothed the crease of his trousers with his forefinger. "Perhaps you would be safe there," he added, "if the Hashashin believed you no longer had the mirror."

"You wouldn't just leave us, would you?" said Maxine, begging him with her eyes.

Grandpa didn't answer but sat silent with his thoughts.

"What makes you think he'll be so eager to trade?" she asked. "Out there in the desert surrounded by all his killers, why will he bargain civilly with you?"

"Yes, well, this is a matter which may require some finesse," Grandpa admitted, "or perhaps the opposite of finesse, whatever that may be. My plan is still being formulated and by the nature of the situation must be somewhat extemporaneous."

The cousins looked skeptical.

"Come, come!" he said with an injured scowl. "I'm not exactly a novice in these matters. I know the desert like the back of my hand. I understand every subtlety of the Hashashin mind. I speak their language and dialects fluently. Rest assured, I am equal to the challenge."

It seemed there was nothing more to discuss. Grandpa was clearly resolved.

"So when are you leaving?" asked William at last.

"The ship sails day after tomorrow."

"Don't go," whispered Maxine.

"Sleep now," said Grandpa, rising from his chair. "We can worry about tomorrow when it comes."

The lights went out, the door closed behind him, and William and Maxine were alone. They were beyond tired, in mind and body, but their thoughts were churning, and despite their exhaustion, they found sleep impossible. A low murmur settled over the darkened room: the faucet dripping in the bath, a chorus of lovesick crickets outside their window, and in the next room a confidential conversation not quite loud enough to decipher.

Something in the tone of Grandpa's and Sufjin's voices lured William from his bed. He took a glass from the bedside table, gulped down the contents, and crept across the room. Warily he pressed the glass to the door and leaned against it. Maxine, disapproving greatly, found her own glass and did the same. The discussion in the next room became audible.

"Do you hear yourself?" said Sufjin. "It is impossible. They barely survived the city."

"They were alone. This would be different. They would be under my supervision."

"Ah yes, well, we may all rest easy then."

"Easy? Not easy, perhaps. Cautiously optimistic."

There was a long silence.

"And what do you suppose their parents would have to say about it?"

"The parents, as you well know, are unavailable for consultation."

"Yes, but perhaps we might make some guess regarding their opinion."

"If pressed on the point, their parents would undoubtedly want the children wherever they are safest."

"And that would be halfway around the world in the middle of the desert, to your way of thinking? The influence of the Hashashin on these shores is a tithe of what you will find across the Mediterranean. You know that better than I."

"The strength of the Cafara is greater there as well. Here they would be unprotected. Vulnerable."

"Then why go? Stay and protect the children. Surely this errand can wait a few weeks."

Silence again.

"You know the answer. What was lost has been found, what I have squandered lies hostage beneath the fortress of Alamut in the Dungeons of Paradise, and now the old jackal loses patience. I must not arrive too late and miss my only chance to mend what I have broken."

William's ear had started to ache from leaning against the water glass. As he shifted his weight the floorboards made a faint creak beneath him. The voices in the next room halted, and the cousins caught their breath and stood stock-still. Before there was even a moment to dive back to their beds, the knob turned and the door sprang open, and William and Maxine sprawled out onto the floor.

"Eavesdropping is thirsty work," said Grandpa. "May I refill your glasses?"

The cousins picked themselves up, and Grandpa folded his arms across his chest. "What did you hear?"

"Not much, really," said William.

"All of it, then, eh?"

They gave him a guilty nod.

"I guessed as much," said Grandpa. He studied them thoughtfully. "So how about it?"

Sufjin shook his head in reproach and turned toward the window.

"How about what?" asked William.

"Are you coming along?" said Grandpa. "I'm offering you the chance to join me on my journey. It seems to me the wisest course. So I ask you again, how about it?"

William cleared his throat uncomfortably. "It sounds pretty dangerous," he said finally.

"Possibly. Though no more dangerous than the alternatives, I suspect. If you stay behind, there is a strong chance the Hashashin will find you eventually, wherever you may be. Persistence is one of their stronger suits. They know your value to me and will use you as pawns to get what they want. And once you have served their purposes . . ."

The cousins stared at each other, their faces pale.

"I'm sorry I've dragged you both into this," said Grandpa, "but now I see only one way out, and that lies in the middle of the desert on the far side of the globe. It's the medicine we must take if we would be free of them.

"But there is a silver lining. It would be the adventure of a lifetime, and for my part, I would choose not to leave my grandchildren behind—the grandchildren I have only now in my old age begun to know. I find I've grown rather fond of you both and have a mind to keep you close by, where I can look after you. And who knows, maybe we will have the chance to leave our mark on one another along the way."

Maxine caught her grandfather's sleeve and clenched it tight. "I don't care about adventure, Grandpa," she said. "And traveling across the ocean in some rat-infested, leaky old boat sounds perfectly awful to me. But I don't want to leave you. I'll follow you wherever you go."

This pierced the old man's heart, and for a moment

his confidence seemed to falter. He scratched his chin and opened his pocket watch, pondering something inside the case, but presently his certainty returned, and he looked to his grandson.

"How about you, my boy? Can I interest you in an adventure?"

"I don't know," said William. "I'm not so sure my parents would care much for the idea."

"They almost certainly would not." Grandpa nodded. "I will answer to them, however."

William's eyes glinted as he pondered the prospect of surveying a shimmering stretch of dunes from the hump of a swaying camel, and the corners of his mouth twitched slightly.

"I'll take that as a yes, then," said Grandpa, ignoring Sufjin's disapproving scowl. "Now it's time for bed. No more hijinks. We have a mountain of preparations to make in the morning."

The Mayfly Inn slept. The world was dark and quiet; even the crickets outside rested from their sonnets. In the delicate stillness Maxine rose from her bed and crossed the room. She raised the window and felt the cool, damp night steal in over the sill; closed her eyes and smelled the silver-leafed cottonwoods, heady-sweet and tart like apple cider. When she opened her eyes again, William was standing beside her, holding the silk-swathed mirror.

"Summer sure got here in a hurry, didn't it?" he said, casually unwinding the black silk ribbon as he watched a host of fireflies wander the meadow between the porch and the lapping water of the lake.

"Is it what you thought it would be?" asked Maxine. "When you showed up on Grandpa's doorstep, did you ever imagine any of this?"

"I guess not," he said with a laugh. "I sort of thought I'd be playing backgammon and bird-watching all summer."

Maxine studied William's face for a moment. "You're as happy as a cricket, aren't you?" she said. "Sailing off into the East like Sinbad, with a pack of wild-eyed killers on your trail."

William cocked his head and grinned.

"Well, that's just swell for you," she said drily. "I guess I shouldn't be surprised—you have the same last name as Grandpa, after all. I'm not sure I'm cut out to play the fearless globe-trotter, though. I was actually kind of excited about spending my summer in the library."

William handed her the mirror. "Sorry, M, but adventuring's in your blood. Like Nura said, we're family. You're a Battersea, too, you know, whether you have the same last name or not. You've proved it a hundred times."

"I have?"

"Well, sure. You outfoxed the White Rat with an ashtray, and stared down the whole temple with a shaving mirror, and stuck a Hashashin with a hat pin for good measure."

"That's a few shy of a hundred. . . ."

"Aw, who's counting, anyways? Besides, you didn't really

want to haunt the library all summer long, did you? I mean, books are fine and all, but who wants to spend their whole life living someone else's story?"

Maxine thought about this for a moment, then pushed her cousin aside. Hoisting herself up onto the windowsill, she dropped to the lawn below.

"Where do you think you're going?"

"Come and find out," she said without looking back.

Maxine walked barefoot down to the water's edge, the long sash of black silk streaming behind her as she went. The mirror was cold and heavy in her hands, and a familiar pall gripped her as her fingers worried the strange eyelets along its outer edge. She sank to the ground, stretching out in the grass and staring up at the night. In the meadow behind, William came trailing after and flopped down beside her so that the tops of their heads were touching, and the fireflies seemed drawn to them and circled like will-o'-wisps round about where they lay.

"Tell us your secret," Maxine murmured, holding the Eye of Midnight to the sky at arm's length, as if it were a celestial compass, the ancient astrolabe of the Orient magi, pointing always east, and they searched there on its surface for some veiled testimony or clue. But the mirror betrayed no confidences, and in its face they saw only their own faces, ghostly pale and luminous in the moonlight, and through its eyelets, a host of stars that burned and swung above in myriad infinite silence, like the stretching sands of Araby's distant shores.

AUTHOR'S NOTE

With certain novels, it is interesting to learn where historical fact has crept in and left its smudgy fingerprints on the fiction. While I suspect my readers would never mistake William and Maxine's encounter with the villainous Hashashin for a history textbook, they might be curious to know which of the details do have their roots in real life.

The truth is, the Hashashin did exist, about a thousand years ago. They were a secret order of trained killers based in a remote hideout near the present-day border of Turkey and Iran, and they carried out the schemes and political plots of a succession of Grandmasters, each of whom went by the colorful title of the Old Man of the Mountain. They were fearless, fanatical, and invisible, and for almost two centuries they were the dread of the Middle Eastern world.

Then, in 1295, a young Italian named Marco Polo returned from an extended vacation to the Far East, bringing back a fascinating and often imaginative narrative of his travels, including one particularly compelling tale involving a desert fortress called Alamut with a hidden garden and a horde of sinister assassins all willing to give their lives unquestionably in the service of their charismatic leader.

Marco Polo's sensational account of the Hashashin quickly captured the imagination of the Western world, but it has raised a multitude of questions from historians: Was there really a secret garden of paradise behind the walls of Alamut? How did the Old Man of the Mountain compel his followers to do his bidding? Were the Hashashin truly villains or simply another faction in the complex fabric of a turbulent time?

When I first read about the legends of the Hashashin, however, my imagination immediately leapt to questions of the "what if" variety. What if the Hashashin were never really stamped out by the Mongols in 1275? What if they only slipped away into the shadows, biding their time, waiting for an opportunity to execute a diabolical plan to conquer the world? And what if, in 1929, they descended, in all their exotic, terrifying, *Arabian Nights* glory, on the unsuspecting populace of New York City?

While the Hashashin and their deadly daggers are no fabrication, the mysterious relic known as the Eye of Midnight is another matter. It is my own invention, and though it has no historical basis, it seems a likely artifact in light of the abundance of magic mirrors in Arabian literature and the Old Man of the Mountain's reputation (among his followers, at least) for mystical powers. The Cafara, the Sons of the Cipher, are a figment of my imagination as well. I found it interesting to suppose that there was another clandestine society—a virtuous fraternity set in opposition to the Ha-shashin, sworn throughout the centuries to stand against the plots of the ruthless sect.

As for New York City, things have changed a fair amount since the Roaring Twenties. The jazz clubs on Fifty-Second Street are gone now. Ellis Island no longer welcomes its huddled masses yearning to breathe free (indeed, even in 1929 this had already become a more seldom occurrence), and alas, that luminous cathedral of Beaux Arts architecture, Old Penn Station, was torn down in 1963 to make way for Madison Square Garden. Those things were all there, though, once upon a time, and I've done my best to re-create the ambience of old Manhattan with reasonable accuracy. There never was a Knickerbocker Plainsong Cemetery, I'm afraid, but you can still visit Cleopatra's Needle on the east side of Central Park, and if you look carefully, perhaps you will find the bench where Nura's satchel was snatched in Battery Park.

And then, of course, there is Colonel Horatius Battersea, a prime specimen of that peculiar breed of swash-buckling explorer, agent provocateur, travel writer, and spy that seemed to abound at the turn of the twentieth century, an era when adventuring was a bona fide occupation. The colonel was inspired by men and women like Lawrence of Arabia, Freya Stark, Sir Richard Francis Burton, and Gertrude Bell—fascinating figures, all of them, and well worth the effort of tracking down for their own exploits and memoirs.

So there it is. A complicated concoction of factual

elements and bald fiction all stirred up in the same caul-
dron. If I've taken any liberties with history, it was always
for the sake of my deep conviction in another truth: that we
are all designed for an adventure, that it lies in every young
heart, and that losing ourselves in the pages of such things,
even for a few hours, may kindle something in our souls that
can never be extinguished.

GLOSSARY

1920s Slang, Idioms, and Terminology

"Applesauce!": "Nonsense!" or "That's absurd!"

bats: Crazy.

billy club: A nightstick often carried by policemen.

blower: A telephone.

bogeyman: A nondescript individual or creature of terror, often invoked to frighten children.

Brylcreem: A brand of popular hair pomade. See *pomade*.

cabbage: Paper money.

Charleston: A fast, spirited popular dance.

cigarillo: A small, thin cigar.

cloche: A close-fitting, bell-shaped woman's hat.

coffin varnish: A term for bootleg alcohol, typically of poor quality, from the period of the Prohibition.

conk: A person's head.

drugstore cowboy: A young man who hangs around on street corners or in drugstores.

Dumb Dora: A phrase from popular culture referring to a dim-witted female.

eight bits: A "bit" is a colloquial term meaning twelve and a half cents. Since no coin exists in this denomination, the term is used in cases of even multiples (e.g., two bits being a quarter, four bits being fifty cents, and eight bits being a dollar).

flappers: A class of women characterized by disregard for traditional norms of dress and behavior.

flat tire: A useless or inept person.

"for the birds": Pointless or useless, of interest only to suckers.

gink: An odd man.

"Go on!": "That's ridiculous!" or "Quit pulling my leg."

"have kittens": To have a fit of anxiety or anticipation.

nighthawk: A person who likes to be out and about late at night.

"Now we're on the trolley!": An expression used when someone finally understands or does something correctly.

plus-fours: A style of baggy trousers reaching below the knee (presumably four inches longer than typical knickers), popular for active pursuits.

pomade: A greasy, perfumed ointment used primarily by men for grooming the hair.

thimblerigger: A swindler who operates a shell game.

Tommy gun: Nickname for the Thompson machine gun, which became infamous for its use by gangsters. Also known as a "Chicago typewriter" or a "chopper."

whelp: A puppy; a smart-aleck.

Foreign Words and Expressions

"Aferin" (AH-fay-rihn, Turkish): "Nice job" or "Well done."

al-kaljin (al-KAHL-jihn): An invented term, meant to be a westernized portmanteau formed by the corruption of a pair of Arabic words (*al-khayl*, "horse," and *jinn*, "hidden ones") used as a designation for a wooden statue that can be brought to life when possessed by a spirit known as a jinni.

Alamut (AH-la-moot, Persian): Literally "the eagle's nest." The desert fortress of the Old Man of the Mountain and the Hashashin, located somewhere between Turkey and Iran.

Ana (ah-NA, Turkish): Mama.

Baba (bah-BA, Turkish): Papa.

bir canavar **(BIHR ja-na-VAR, Turkish):** An ogre or monster.

diwan (dee-WAN, Arabic): A sheaf of papers; more specifically, a collection of poetry.

djambia **(JAM-bee-yah, Arabic):** The chosen weapon of the Hashashin, a long dagger with a distinctive backward-curving blade.

effendi **(ih-FEN-dee, Turkish):** A title of honor and respect.

fida'i **(fi-dah-EE, Arabic):** Literally "the sacrificial ones." A plural or singular term for the trained assassins within the Hashashin order.

gorunmeyen **(GOO-roon-MAY-en, Turkish):** Unseen, invisible.

"Hist!" **(HEESHT, Turkish):** "Shush!"

jinni (JIH-nee, Arabic): In Arabian mythology, a spirit or demon with an essence of scorching fire.

"Marhaba" **(MAHR-ha-bah, Arabic):** "Hello" (an informal greeting).

Rafiq (rah-FEEK, Arabic): The highest rank within the Hashashin order, bestowed on the members of the inner circle of the Old Man of the Mountain, who commands the fida'i in the Old Man's absence.

sadiqi **(SAH-dee-kee, Arabic):** friend.

"Tasharrafna" **(tah-shah-RAHF-nah, Arabic):** "A pleasure to meet you." Literally "You honor us."

"Vay canina!" **(WHY JAH-NEE-nah, Turkish):** An interjection expressing disbelief, along the lines of "Oh brother!" or "You've got to be kidding!"

Miscellany

Araby (from French): A poetic term for the geographic area historically called Arabia.

astrolabe (from Greek): An archaic instrument used in astronomy, to take altitudes and measure the position of the stars.

cassock (corruption of Arabic): A close-fitting ankle-length frock or tunic.

diabolus (Latin): A devil, demon.

divan (from Persian): An eastern-style low bed or couch, furnished with cushions.

hubble-bubble: An eastern-style water pipe for smoking tobacco, also known as a hookah or shisha.

jackal (corruption of Turkish): A long-eared member of the dog family that hunts in the desert by night.

kohl (Arabic): In the East, a dark black powder prepared from iron sulfide, applied to the eyelids for cosmetic, health-related, or mystical purposes.

magi (from Persian): Historically, members of an ancient Persian priestly class; more broadly, magicians or astrologers of the East.

moniker (obscure origins): A name or nickname.

obolus (Latin): A silver coin referred to by ancient Greek writers when describing the toll required by Charon, who ferried souls across the river Styx to the land of the dead.

portcullis (from French): A heavy grate, formed of horizontal and vertical iron bars, spiked on the bottom and suspended by ropes or chains in order to be lowered quickly to defend a gateway against an assault.

scimitar (obscure origins): A curved sword with a single edge, used predominantly by the Turks and Persians.

windlass (obscure origins): A mechanism consisting of a wheel with hand spokes set on a horizontal axle, around which a rope is spooled for the purpose of hoisting heavy weights.

ACKNOWLEDGMENTS

It takes a village, I think, to make a book. My particular village is a charming one, inhabited by some of the most talented, supportive, long-suffering people I could ever hope to know.

Deep appreciation to my amazing agent, Danielle Chiotti, who has tirelessly held her lantern aloft to guide me through the perilous spheres of the world of publishing, and to my wonderful editor, Rebecca Weston, who understood the story I wanted to create and had the insight and imagination to make it come to life. We did this together.

Compliments and recognition as well to all the wonderful people at Delacorte Press and Random House who made the publication of this book possible, and to Kate Welch, who plucked my manuscript from obscurity and the query pile at Upstart Crow Literary.

To my friends Dan Haase and Skye Jethani, who subjected my chapters to the crucible and convinced me to share Maxine and William's adventures with a broader audience— it's a pleasure and a privilege to walk the journey with you.

Heartfelt gratitude to everyone else I foisted this book on, when it was still definitely not ready for prime time—to Todd Martin, Ken Kunz, Rachel Rusin, David and Renee Brumbach, and Colonel Dave Oleson; to my grandmother Maxine Brumbach, who I'm certain lent more to my heroine than just her name; and to five particular young people—my boys, Jacob and Drew, and Katie Chamberlain, Jackson Elliot, and Chris Haase. It was their enthusiastic responses to this book that allowed me to hope it could connect with the adventuresome hearts it was intended for.

Most especially, love and thanks to my wife, Lisa, who supplied the space and endless encouragement I needed to see this book through to the finish, and to my mom and dad, who still tell me I can be whatever I want to be when I grow up.

ABOUT THE AUTHOR

Andrew Brumbach grew up square in the hippie community of Eugene, Oregon, surrounded by artists and musicians and storytellers. He studied art in Texas, traded bond options in Chicago, and spent a few years lost in the neon neighborhoods of Tōkyo. Somewhere along the way, he married the girl of his dreams and had four practically perfect kids, but he never overcame his weakness for the power and transport of story. Now he lives in suburban Illinois but secretly daydreams about chasing bandits across the desert with Lawrence of Arabia and Gertrude Bell under cloudless, starry skies. *The Eye of Midnight* is his first novel.

Visit Andrew at AndrewBrumbach.com.